PURRDLE

About the Authors

Dr Gareth Moore is the internationally bestselling author of a wide range of brain-training and puzzle books for children and adults. His books have sold millions of copies in the UK alone, and have been published in over thirty languages. He is also the creator of online brain-training site BrainedUp.com, and runs the daily puzzle site PuzzleMix.com.

Web: DrGarethMoore.com
Twitter/X: @DrGarethMoore
YouTube: YouTube.com/@DrGareth

Laura Jayne Ayres is a puzzle writer and author. She studied Linguistics at the University of Cambridge and is also a published playwright.

Also by the Authors

Meowdle
Woofdle
The Great British Puzzle Book
The Highway Code Puzzle Book
The Whodunnit Puzzle Book
The Murder Mystery Club Puzzle Book: The Murder in the Village
The Murder Mystery Club Puzzle Book: The Perfect Plot
The Undercover Agent Puzzle Book
The Natural History Puzzle Book
The Astrology Puzzle Book
The Movie Puzzle Book

With brands

Spydle (with The National Archives)
The BBC Puzzle Book
The British Museum Puzzle Book
The British Army Challenge Book
The Transport for London Puzzle Book
The FIFA Football Puzzle Book
The RAF Association Puzzle Book
IFLScience! Puzzle Book
RHS Puzzles & Brain Teasers
RSPB Garden Birdwatcher's Puzzle Book
The Ordnance Survey Kids' Adventure Book

A PURR-ODY

75 MORE FELINE CRIME PUZZLES TO SOLVE USING LOGIC, SKILL & THE POWER OF CATNAPS

PURRDLE

DR GARETH MOORE & LAURA JAYNE AYRES

AUTHORS OF *MEOWDLE*

greenfinch

First published in Great Britain in 2025 by Greenfinch
An imprint of Quercus
Part of John Murray Group

A CIP catalogue record for this book is available from the British Library

PB ISBN 978-1-52944-777-4
eBook ISBN 978-1-52944-778-1

10 9 8 7 6 5 4 3 2 1

Cover design by Matt Burne
Printed and bound in Great Britain by Clays Ltd, Elcograf S.p.A.

MIX
Paper | Supporting responsible forestry
FSC® C104740

Papers used by Quercus are from well-managed forests and other responsible sources.

Quercus
Carmelite House
50 Victoria Embankment
London EC4Y 0DZ

John Murray Group
Part of Hodder & Stoughton Limited
An Hachette UK company

The authorised representative in the EEA is Hachette Ireland, 8 Castlecourt Centre, Dublin 15, D15 XTP3, Ireland (email: info@hbgi.ie)

Contents

Instructions

Welcome to *Purrdle*: a book for cat lovers, for victims of cat crime, and for the very large overlap between those two groups.

Work out who did what during 75 cattily criminal cases, drawing careful conclusions from the clues.

For each case, read the situation and then consider the bulleted set of clues. Combine these bulleted clues with the information in the chart on the following page, which lists all of the possible options for each cat. No two cats in the same case will ever use the same option, so once you assign something to a cat then you *know for certain* that none of the other cats match that option.

As you work out who did – or didn't – do things, mark this on the chart. Tick intersecting boxes when things match, and put a cross in those same boxes when they *don't* match.

Collate information in the table, and use the table when solving too – not just for keeping track of your conclusions.

And, once all is done, you should be able to answer the **bold question** in each case.

The full breakdown of who did what in every case is given in the solution section at the back of the book, with the cat that answers the bold question highlighted with a shaded background. Good luck!

Dr Gareth Moore	Laura Jayne Ayres

Chapter 1

Playful Pusses

1. Unwelcome Guests

Megan, Shania and Annie the Anarchist have always been the sole pet in their respective homes. In a baffling move, each of their owners has brought home a new animal friend – presumably as an act of malice. Naturally, the cats have extremely strong views on their owners' new friends and have decided to respond in the manner they know best: with extreme pettiness.

Work out which cat has been affronted by which new animal, and what each retaliatory move was.

The cat who promptly ran away from home will, in fact, return in two hours and demand, incessantly, to be fed. Who was it?

- Annie the Anarchist smashed a vase
- The appearance of the goldfish did not induce the curtain-pulling-down incident
- Shania was not the cat offended by the gecko
- Whoever pulled down the curtains wasn't upset about a dog (this time)
- Annie the Anarchist was either offended by a dog or by a gecko

		Pet			Retaliation		
		Dog	Gecko	Goldfish	Pulled down curtains	Ran away	Smashed vase
Cat	Annie the Anarchist						
	Megan						
	Shania						
Retaliation	Pulled down curtains						
	Ran away						
	Smashed vase						

Cat	Pet	Retaliation

2. Not Now, Thanks

Claudio, Braun and Madam MacAdams are all extremely independent cats who require no additional human attention, thank you very much. Their owners are bafflingly insistent that the cats interact with them, and will do anything to force affection. On this particular day, the cats have all been minding their own businesses in their favourite nap spots, and their owners have tried to lure them into some sort of playful episode with a new toy.

Work out which cat has been napping in which spot, and what toy they have been offered.

The cat who was napping in the bathtub did not only ignore the new toy, but actually pretended not to hear their owner at all. Who was it?

- Claudio was being harassed with a feather toy
- Braun was trying to nap on top of the fridge
- The cat who was offered a scratch post was either Madam MacAdams or the cat trying to nap on the shoe rack – but not both

		Location			Toy		
		Bathtub	Shoe rack	Top of fridge	Bells	Feather	Scratch post
Cat	Braun						
	Claudio						
	Madam MacAdams						
Toy	Bells						
	Feather						
	Scratch post						

Cat	Location	Toy

3. The Ins and Outs

Adrian, Emerald and Lady Puffball are adventurous cats who have spent an afternoon outside in the sunshine, and have signalled that their exterior excursions have come to an end. All three cats have then waited outside the back door and notified their owners in their own ways that they would like to be readmitted to their houses. When the door was opened, however, the capricious cats then decided that they would prefer to undertake another outdoor activity and abandoned the newly opened portals.

Work out which cat notified their owners in what way, and what activity they then pursued outside instead of coming in.

The cat who decided to be a general menace will later bring a live mouse into the house, when they eventually decide to come in. Who was it?

- Adrian either wanted to chase butterflies or dig up vegetables
- The cat who went on to be a general menace had either tried headbutting the door, or was Emerald – but not both
- Whoever wanted to chase butterflies had been doing some meowing outside first
- Emerald scampered off to dig up some vegetables

		Notification			Activity		
		Headbutting door	Meowing	Scratching door	Be a general menace	Chase butterflies	Dig up vegetables
Cat	Adrian						
	Emerald						
	Lady Puffball						
Activity	Be a general menace						
	Chase butterflies						
	Dig up vegetables						

Cat	Notification	Activity

4. Pamper Session

Saoirse, Velma and Mini Minnie are calm kitties who have decided to treat their owners to an unexpected spa session. The chief component of the treatment involves incessantly licking a body part belonging to their human owner, whether or not they requested it. The cats have also thrown in an additional extra motion to add to the soothing atmosphere of the spa, which was better-received than the exfoliating licking.

Work out which cat licked which of their owners' body parts, and what soothing extra they added in.

The cat who nuzzled their owner will, unfortunately, undo the soothing effects of the spa by throwing up on their owner's lap in a few moments. Who was it?

- Saoirse licked her owner's toes (incessantly)
- Velma was not the nuzzler
- Whoever added some nuzzling was not the cat who had licked their owner's head (incessantly)
- Mini Minnie was not the cat who had (incessantly) been licking elbows
- The cat who had licked their owner's elbows, however, was not the same one who did some extra purring

		Body part			Soothing extra		
		Elbows	Head	Toes	Cuddling	Nuzzling	Purring
Cat	Mini Minnie						
	Saoirse						
	Velma						
Soothing extra	Cuddling						
	Nuzzling						
	Purring						

Cat	Body part	Soothing extra

5. The Last Supper

Hermione, Tycho and Lionel Scritchie enjoy spending time in the kitchen with their loved ones. Unfortunately for their loved ones, however, the three cats have taken serious offence to the meals that their human owners have prepared for themselves, and swiped them from the countertop onto the floor. The meals have each landed with an almighty crash, shattering the plates they were on along with the hopes of the chefs. The cats, however, don't seem to be sharing in the despair.

Work out which cat swiped which plate of food, and what their motive seems to have been.

The cat who acted out of spite will, to add insult to injury, eat some of the discarded food while making eye contact with its sad chef. Who was it?

- Hermione hadn't acted out of insouciance (for a change), and neither had Lionel Scritchie
- The cat who swiped the spaghetti did so out of boredom
- Tycho was not the swiper of the Irish stew
- Lionel Scritchie hadn't acted out of boredom

		Food			Motive		
		Irish stew	Roast lamb	Spaghetti	Boredom	Insouciance	Spite
Cat	Hermione						
	Lionel Scritchie						
	Tycho						
Motive	Boredom						
	Insouciance						
	Spite						

Cat	Food	Motive

6. Horticultural Horror

Angelica, Forrest and Tortoiseshell Tim have been helping their owners in the garden, all of whom are keen vegetable growers. In their attempts to assist, however, the cats have all been spooked by a recently harvested veggie which they were momentarily convinced was a serious threat, akin to a venomous viper or similar. The cats would argue that they did not overreact at all, but their responses were certainly on the hysterical side of dramatic.

Work out which cat was spooked by what vegetable, and how they reacted.

The cat who was spooked by the cucumber also sank their claws into it, for good measure. Who was it?

- Whoever hissed, hissed at a cucumber
- Forrest was not the cat who responded with yelping
- The runner bean spooked either Forrest or Angelica
- Angelica was the hissing kitty

		Reaction			Vegetable		
		Hissing	Spitting	Yelping	Broccoli	Cucumber	Runner bean
Cat	Angelica						
	Forrest						
	Tortoiseshell Tim						
Vegetable	Broccoli						
	Cucumber						
	Runner bean						

Cat	Reaction	Vegetable

7. Friends in High Places

Cecily, Indiana and Meredith Blake are all daredevils, who know no fear and know no danger. Their adventurous attitudes have, unfortunately, run them into a spot of bother: the three cats are now stuck on the roofs of mid-rise buildings, and will require emergency intervention to bring them down. Determined to keep their cool, the kitties will later display non-remorseful attitudes when they are finally rescued.

Work out which cat was stuck on what height of building, and what their attitude will be upon rescue.

The cat who got stuck on the highest building will attempt to attack the person coming to the rescue. Who was it?

- Meredith Blake was feeling defiant
- Indiana was not feeling nonchalant
- Whoever was feeling unconcerned was doing so at the top of a seven-storey building
- The five-storey building was not the one scaled by Meredith Blake

		Number of storeys			Reaction		
		5	7	12	Defiant	Nonchalant	Unconcerned
Cat	Cecily						
	Indiana						
	Meredith Blake						
Reaction	Defiant						
	Nonchalant						
	Unconcerned						

Cat	Number of storeys	Reaction

8. A Clean Sleep

Savannah, Calypso and Cindy Clawford are three chilled-out kitties, who just love to take a little snooze in a sunny spot on a quiet day. Today, the three cats have curled up and snuggled into what they believe to be a perfectly acceptable place for a kip: on top of a pile of newly laundered clothes. The item of clothing of top of each pile has thus become covered in cat hairs, all of which are different colours. The cats do not care, because they are asleep. And are cats.

Work out which cat napped on which item of clothing, and what colour hairs they have left all over it.

The cat who left black hairs on their laundry pile has also added a few dusty paw prints into the mix. Who was it?

- Savannah hadn't napped on a dress shirt
- Cindy Clawford didn't have grey hairs
- The black hairs weren't found on the pyjamas, and nor were the pyjamas napped on by Savannah
- The Y-fronts were not adorned with grey hairs
- The pyjamas either had ginger or black hairs on them

		Clothing			Hair colour		
		Dress shirt	Pyjamas	Y-fronts	Black	Ginger	Grey
Cat	Calypso						
	Cindy Clawford						
	Savannah						
Hair colour	Black						
	Ginger						
	Grey						

Cat	Clothing	Hair colour

9. Hide and Sneak

Cormac, Flash and Dr Watson are all masters of disguise, who move silently through their realms and keep a low profile. So surreptitious are the kitties that today their owners briefly wondered if they had escaped the house forever, despite all three cats being sound asleep in a hiding spot upstairs. Being good sports, the cats emerged from their sleeps just as their owners were about to print off 'Missing' posters, and demanded their favourite foods for dinner.

Work out which cat was hiding in which spot, and what they demanded for supper.

The cat who was hiding in the laundry basket actually pulled some of the clothes over themselves, like a blanket, to deepen the subterfuge. Who was it?

- Cormac demanded tuna for supper
- Whoever had hidden in the laundry basket was not the one who demanded chicken
- Whoever hid in the bread bin later demanded salmon
- Dr Watson wasn't the cat hiding behind the TV

		Hiding spot			Food		
		Behind TV	Bread bin	Laundry basket	Chicken	Salmon	Tuna
Cat	Cormac						
	Dr Watson						
	Flash						
Food	Chicken						
	Salmon						
	Tuna						

Cat	Hiding spot	Food

10. Insistent Assistance

Lorelei, Pebbles and Spotty Simone are extremely friendly cats who show their affection by literally never leaving their owners alone for a single second. On this occasion, the three cats have followed their owners into a room where they are trying to undertake a small, but important, task, which the cats are assisting with by putting their heads directly in front of their owners' faces. Their owners may or may not be desperate for alone time, but they really should have thought about that before getting a cat.

Work out which cat is in what room, and which task they're assisting with.

The cat who helped with signing the mortgage deeds instead guaranteed that the task would need to be done all over again. Who was it?

- Lorelei wasn't in the office, and nor was she helping with the mortgage deeds
- Whoever was trying to sign the mortgage deeds wasn't doing so in the kitchen
- The bathroom was either the location of the important phone call or the mortgage deed signing
- Spotty Simone was helping in the kitchen

		Location			Task		
		Bathroom	Kitchen	Office	Important phone call	Signing mortgage deeds	Treating minor injury
Cat	Lorelei						
	Pebbles						
	Spotty Simone						
Task	Important phone call						
	Signing mortgage deeds						
	Treating minor injury						

Cat	Location	Task

11. Unintended Invitees

Gabriel, Topaz and The Whiskered Wonder are curious cats who love to explore their surroundings. Today, the cats have flexed their adventurous muscles by exploring the homes of some other residents on their street, where the homeowners have been foolish enough to leave an opening just wide enough for the cats to use as an entrance. Unfortunately, the explorers all gave the game away themselves, and were shooed out when the evidence of their trespass was discovered.

Work out which cat broke in through which aperture, and the evidence they left behind.

The cat who entered through the door also brought a few muddy paw prints in with them. Who was it?

- Whoever used the door is not the cat who left hairs everywhere
- Gabriel either snuck in through the window or left hairs everywhere – but not both
- The Whiskered Wonder managed to knock over a plant pot during her escapade
- Topaz was not the clandestine meower

		Entrance			Evidence		
		Cat flap	Door	Window	Hairs everywhere	Knocked over plant pot	Meow
Cat	Gabriel						
	The Whiskered Wonder						
	Topaz						
Evidence	Hairs everywhere						
	Knocked over plant pot						
	Meow						

Cat	Entrance	Evidence

12. An Important Interruption

Maura, Raddix and The Enigma are amiable cats who just love to spend time in company. The most recent manifestation of this desire has involved the cats desperately clawing at their owners' closed bathroom doors while their human friends attempt to go about their business. Not happy with being ignored, each cat has chosen a different method of communicating their emotions, which are all equally strong.

Work out which cat communicated in which way, and what their feelings were.

The cat who expressed concern mitigated the caring gesture by biting their owner's toes when the door was finally unlocked. Who was it?

- Whoever was crying at the bathroom door was either The Enigma or the cat feeling disappointment – but not both
- Raddix was neither yowling nor feeling concern
- The feeling of desolation was communicated by a crying cat

		Communication			Feelings		
		Crying	Whining	Yowling	Concern	Desolation	Disappointment
Cat	Maura						
	Raddix						
	The Enigma						
Feelings	Concern						
	Desolation						
	Disappointment						

Cat	Communication	Feelings

13. Silent Menace

Vance, Storm and Catchu Picchu are snuggly cats who have snuck into bed with their owners for a dreamy, snoozy cuddle. The cats have all curled themselves into an extremely cosy position which just happens to be directly on the face of their human friends, preventing them from breathing and threatening them with imminent demise. For some reason, the cats have thence been exiled from the bedrooms and have been forced to work through their ensuing emotions alone.

Work out which cat was banished to which room, and what emotion they felt when they arrived there.

The cat experiencing emotions of defiance would manage to find their way back to their owner's bedroom to repeat the offence. Who was it?

- Vance was either feeling defiant or surprised
- Whatever Vance was feeling, he was feeling it in the living room
- The cat in the kitchen was not the one feeling feelings of disappointment
- Catchu Picchu was feeling surprised at their exile

		Exile			Emotion		
		Bathroom	Kitchen	Living room	Defiance	Disappointment	Surprise
Cat	Catchu Picchu						
	Storm						
	Vance						
Emotion	Defiance						
	Disappointment						
	Surprise						

Cat	Exile	Emotion

14. Meditation Retreat

Catterin the Great, Asterix and Baroness Bertha have all decided that they need a moment to themselves, and have clambered into a cool, dark cupboard to be alone with their thoughts. To their great surprise, the cats cannot open the doors from the inside, and have been stuck there for some time. On the plus side, all three cats have now had plenty of time to plot their revenge for when they finally escape – even though they are the sole architects of their situations.

Work out which cat clambered into which cupboard, and how long they spent in there before escaping.

The cat who was trapped in the coat closet found a nice pair of mittens and clawed them to pieces to pass the time. Who was it?

- The cat stuck for just one hour was either in the coat closet or was Baroness Bertha – but not both
- The cat that was stuck for two hours was not Asterix – and nor was it Baroness Bertha
- The cat stuck for just one hour was not in the laundry cupboard
- The cat that was stuck for two hours was holed up in the pantry, which at least was an interesting place to be

		Cupboard			Time spent		
		Coat closet	Laundry cupboard	Pantry	30 minutes	1 hour	2 hours
Cat	Asterix						
	Baroness Bertha						
	Catterin the Great						
Time spent	30 minutes						
	1 hour						
	2 hours						

Cat	Cupboard	Time spent

15. Bug Bearers

Madonna, Knox and Quickstep Sally are open-minded omnivores who are always keen to try out new local cuisines. They have each expanded their palates by bringing home a large insect, and have proceeded to dismantle it in the homes of their horrified owners. The cats don't understand the appalled shrieks, especially as the cats made sure to decapitate the bugs fully before playing with them, as an act of kindness. They're not *monsters*, after all.

Work out which cat brought in which insect, and what evidence was left on the kitchen floor when finished.

The cat who brought in a cockroach will be banished outside for several hours – but alas, this will only encourage their culinary pursuits. Who was it?

- Madonna did not bring in the cockroach
- The grasshopper was not the insect identified by an antenna
- The bumblebee was either brought in by Knox or left behind a leg as evidence – but not both
- Knox did not leave an antenna behind as evidence
- The wing was not left behind by a grasshopper

		Insect			Evidence		
		Bumblebee	Cockroach	Grasshopper	Antenna	Leg	Wing
Cat	Knox						
	Madonna						
	Quickstep Sally						
Evidence	Antenna						
	Leg						
	Wing						

Cat	Insect	Evidence

16. One Fell Swoop

Crystal, Fergal and Nine Lives Lisa have each been out for a stroll on their neighbourhood rooftops, taking in the sunny views and the good vibes. Distracted by the joys of nature, the cats have taken a wrong step and accidentally fallen into the house of a stranger through an open skylight. Physically, the felines are fine, but emotionally they are wounded. The cats have destroyed one item in each room as an act of retribution, despite the fact that their only enemies are gravity, and themselves.

Work out which cat fell into which room, and what they chose to destroy there.

The cat who fell into the bathroom had the added insult of falling directly into a recently drawn bubble bath. Who was it?

- The bathrobe was destroyed by Crystal
- Whoever fell into the office destroyed a soft cushion
- Fergal either destroyed a laptop, or fell into the bathroom – but not both

		Room			Destroyed item		
		Bathroom	Bedroom	Office	Bathrobe	Laptop	Soft cushion
Cat	Crystal						
	Fergal						
	Nine Lives Lisa						
Destroyed item	Bathrobe						
	Laptop						
	Soft cushion						

Cat	Room	Destroyed item

17. Big Tools

Lorenzo, Aqua and Mr Big take pride in their homes and gardens, and can frequently be found perfecting the layout of the outdoor plant beds by digging up the plants and distributing them around the lawn. Strangely, their owners don't appreciate the unscheduled landscape gardening, and have got out some tools to try and 'rectify' the situation. The cats not only despise this feedback, but are also seriously afraid of the tools in question, adding more insult to injury.

Work out which cat dug up what plant, and which tool they were spooked by.

The cat who was spooked by the garden hose jumped so far that they flattened another plant in the process. Who was it?

- Mr Big was not the cat spooked by the rake
- Whoever was bamboozled by the hose had been digging up a sage plant
- Aqua hadn't been digging up the rosemary plant
- The lavender plant was either dug up by Lorenzo or by the cat who was spooked by the hose – but not both

		Plant			Tool		
		Lavender	Rosemary	Sage	Hose	Rake	Spade
Cat	Aqua						
	Lorenzo						
	Mr Big						
Tool	Hose						
	Rake						
	Spade						

Cat	Plant	Tool

18. Sworn Enemies

Ariel, Cinnabar and Alexander Hameowlton have been dealing with one of life's greatest tribulations: a new cat on the block. Each of their neighbours has had the audacity to introduce a tiny new kitten to their homes, and the three original cats are having none of it. They have each planned out an act of malice to let the new kitties know where they stand, though the kittens are not yet allowed to explore outside so the messages were conveyed through a ground-floor window. The cats are confident that this did not diminish the seriousness of the message in any way.

Work out which cat has taken offence to which kitten and what malicious act it was that they tried to convey through the window.

The cat who tried to headbutt the window certainly caused more harm to themselves than anyone else. Who was it?

- Cinnabar had taken to harassing Muffin
- Whoever had taken offence to Cloudberry was doing a lot of headbutting to make their feelings clear
- The staring contest was instigated by Alexander Hameowlton

		Kitten: Cloudberry	Kitten: Muffin	Kitten: Peaches	Malicious act: Catcalling	Malicious act: Headbutting	Malicious act: Staring contest
Cat	Alexander Hameowlton						
	Ariel						
	Cinnabar						
Malicious act	Catcalling						
	Headbutting						
	Staring contest						

Cat	Kitten	Malicious act

19. Wakey Wakey

Melody, Sorrel and The Princess of Everything are pampered cats who are used to getting their way, whatever their way may be. Day or night, their demands will be met if they meow loud enough, and tonight is no exception. The cats have all woken up their owners in the wee small hours to inform them of their latest wants and needs, and are frankly baffled that their human attendants aren't more thrilled at the prospect of proving themselves useful.

Work out which cat woke their owner up at which time, and what they demanded.

The cat who demanded attention will, in fact, abandon their sleepy owner just as their wishes are about to be granted. Who was it?

- Sorrel made her feelings known at 3am
- The Princess of Everything specifically wanted treats
- Melody either wanted cuddles or wanted something at 2am – but not both
- Either way, Melody was not in the market for attention

		Time			Demand		
		2am	3am	Midnight	Attention	Cuddles	Treats
Cat	Melody						
	Sorrel						
	The Princess of Everything						
Demand	Attention						
	Cuddles						
	Treats						

Cat	Time	Demand

20. At Your Service

Esther, Marigold and Dainty Dido love to help around the house, and especially enjoy adding value in group settings such as dinner parties and celebratory gatherings. For tonight's special, the cats have each provided their assistance by clearing the table, niftily taking a tablecloth in their paws and pulling it off the table in one fell swoop. The fact that the plates had been fully laden and the meal was about to begin is a minor detail, which requires no further scrutiny, thank you very much.

Work out which cat pulled off which tablecloth, and how many plates they each smashed in the process.

The cat who smashed the greatest number of plates helped themselves to a few mouthfuls of the spilled food, by way of payment. Who was it?

- The checked tablecloth was either pulled off by Dainty Dido or by the smasher of exactly six plates – but not both
- Esther did not pull off the checked tablecloth
- The plain tablecloth was either swiped by Marigold, or the cat who smashed ten plates – but not both
- Esther smashed precisely six plates (and was thrilled about it)

		Pattern			Plates smashed		
		Checked	Plain	Striped	6	9	10
Cat	Dainty Dido						
	Esther						
	Marigold						
Plates smashed	6						
	9						
	10						

Cat	Pattern	Plates smashed

21. There's No Limit

Poppy, Sapphire and Harry Houdini are usually cool cats who pride themselves on being calm and collected. They are not immune to bouts of the zoomies, however, and have all spent the last half an hour racing around their houses causing maximum chaos and cacophony. Several items have been broken in the process, but the cats are frankly incapacitated by the thrill of zooming and deeply unbothered. When the moment passes they will be too nonchalant to care, so why fuss now?

Work out which cat broke what item, and which additional symptom of the zoomies they each displayed.

The cat who smashed a lamp only narrowly avoided causing themself an injury. Who was it?

- The cat who broke the lamp was either turbo-purring or chasing a tail
- Sapphire had engaged in a bout of tail chasing
- Poppy was the turbo-purrer
- Whoever broke the television was not the cat who opted for intense staring
- The lamp smasher was not turbo-purring

		Broken item			Additional symptom		
		Lamp	Television	Vase	Intense staring	Tail chasing	Turbo-purring
Cat	Harry Houdini						
	Poppy						
	Sapphire						
Additional symptom	Intense staring						
	Tail chasing						
	Turbo-purring						

Cat	Broken item	Additional symptom

22. Lost in Translation

Dwight, Moses and Professor Nibbles are academic cats, who pride themselves on being in the know. Their main source of knowledge comes from sitting in on their owners' important video calls, in some cases literally. Today, the cats have not only each interrupted a critical conversation but have also sat on their owners' keyboards in such a specific way that they have managed to change the language of the computers being used. Needless to say, the cats are unbothered about this, as the only language they know is one of love and mild chaos.

Work out which cat interrupted which call, and what language they reset the computer to.

The cat who changed the language to Japanese will be in the most trouble, but will care the least. Who was it?

- The computer changed to Japanese had either been engaged in a call about a new job or was changed by Dwight – but not both
- Dwight hadn't disrupted a call from the doctor's office, anyway
- Professor Nibbles changed one language to Norwegian
- The call from the bank was not interrupted by a cat installing Japanese

		Call with			Language		
		Bank	Doctor's office	New job	Japanese	Norwegian	Spanish
Cat	Dwight						
	Moses						
	Professor Nibbles						
Language	Japanese						
	Norwegian						
	Spanish						

Cat	Call with	Language

23. Time to Play

Asher, Elektra and Butch Cassidy are soulful cats who have been moved to create art as a means of expression. Specifically, the three felines have decided to play the musical instruments which their owners have so carelessly left lying around the house, which are simply an invitation to act upon their artistic impulses. The fact that all three instruments feature strings, very similar to the balls of wool they usually enjoy playing with, is neither here nor there, and should not detract from their genius.

Work out which cat attempted to play what instrument, and their corresponding emotions during their concertos.

The cat who played the violin later got their claws tangled in the strings, and a discordant symphony ensued. Who was it?

- Butch Cassidy enjoyed feelings of triumphalism
- Whoever played the violin was feeling jubilant – at least initially
- Triumphalism was not felt by the cat playing the piano
- Elektra wasn't the cat overcome by feelings of perturbation

		Instrument			Feeling		
		Guitar	Piano	Violin	Jubilation	Perturbation	Triumphalism
Cat	Asher						
	Butch Cassidy						
	Elektra						
Feeling	Jubilation						
	Perturbation						
	Triumphalism						

Cat	Instrument	Feeling

24. Attention, Please

Gemma, Aurora and Cosmic Craig are thoroughly independent cats who don't rely on the validation of others to boost their self-esteem. That being said, they have each spent the last half an hour desperately trying to capture their owner's attention so that they might pet, stroke and adore them. When the attention was finally awarded, all three cats naturally shot off to engage in a different activity entirely, so as not to give off the impression of neediness.

Work out which cat employed which method of notification, and what they immediately moved onto.

The cat who decided to subsequently rip up the carpet would soon be banished from their owner's sight altogether. Who was it?

- Aurora had either engaged in some nuzzling or went off to chase dust – but not both
- Cosmic Craig had been yowling (loudly)
- Whoever went on to chew slippers had initially been purring (also loudly)

		Notification			Follow-up activity		
		Nuzzling	Purring	Yowling	Chasing dust	Chewing slippers	Ripping up carpet
Cat	Aurora						
	Cosmic Craig						
	Gemma						
Follow-up activity	Chasing dust						
	Chewing slippers						
	Ripping up carpet						

Cat	Notification	Follow-up activity

25. Laundry Service

Howard, Maximus and Rambo the Rogue love to lend a helping hand, and laundry day is no exception. The three pets have all ignored a lifetime of warnings and quickly snuck behind the open door of a washing machine to have a nice chill-out chewing session on the laundry sitting inside, of which all three loads are in distinct states of cleanliness. Luckily, the cats themselves were never in danger but, alas, three wardrobe staples have been destroyed beyond repair during the cats' domestic downtime.

Work out which cat hopped into which load of laundry, and what item they chewed while in there.

The cat who pulled apart a woollen jumper also managed to leave long hairs all over the laundry in the machine. Who was it?

- Maximus either hopped onto the just-washed laundry or sunk his teeth into a woollen jumper – but not both
- The woollen jumper was not in the dry laundry pile
- Howard was not the cat chewing on the unwashed laundry
- Maximus cheerfully chewed on some pyjamas

		Laundry state			Chewed item		
		Dry	Just-washed	Unwashed	Pyjamas	Underpants	Woollen jumper
Cat	Howard						
	Maximus						
	Rambo the Rogue						
Chewed item	Pyjamas						
	Underpants						
	Woollen jumper						

Cat	Laundry state	Chewed item

Chapter 2

Puzzling Pusses

26. Midnight Feast

Linford, Truman and Sneaky St James spent a relaxing evening at home last night, scratching at the door and yowling at their owners until they released them into the wild. All three cats had openly ignored the food which had been lovingly prepared for them, and instead opted to hunt for a midnight snack. To their owners' despair, all three snacks were brought home quite alive, and then dumped on their beds – very close to their sleeping faces. For some reason, the cats' culinary catches haven't been well-received, which must be down to a general lack of refinement in the human palate.

Work out which cat left through what door, which dinner they ignored, and what animal they brought home with them. **The cat who brought in a bat is a public menace who has received cautions for this behaviour previously. Who was it?**

- Linford either snuck out of the front door or ignored a dish of beef – but not both
- The frog was either brought in by Linford or the cat who ignored some chicken – but not both
- Truman had not ignored a dish of chicken
- Whoever ignored the fish was not the cat who brought in a bird, and nor did they bring in the bat
- The cat who snuck out of the back door hadn't ignored a supper of beef on the way

- The bird-bringer was not Sneaky St James

		Door			Animal			Dinner ignored		
		Back	Front	Side	Bat	Bird	Frog	Beef	Chicken	Fish
Cat	Linford									
	Sneaky St James									
	Truman									
Dinner ignored	Beef									
	Chicken									
	Fish									
Animal	Bat									
	Bird									
	Frog									

Cat	Door	Dinner ignored	Animal

27. Feeling Touchy

Amanda, Billie Jean and Dame Delilah are golden oldies. Their owners, however, are still acting as though they've never met a cat before, because all three kitties have just been stroked on a body part which they did not want to be petted on today. Ignoring the fact that this perceived offence is brand new and yesterday would not have caused an issue, all three cats have issued a scathing response to their bewildered owners, and have even taken the time to cause additional damage to a household object to really get the point across.

Work out which cat was petted on which (incorrect) body part, how they responded, and what additional object they destroyed. **The cat who destroyed the feather cushion was planning to do so any way, and her implied rage was simply a ruse. Who was it?**

- Neither Amanda nor Dame Delilah bit anyone
- Whoever chose biting wasn't offended by ear pets
- The cat incorrectly petted on their nose broke a water jug in retribution
- Billie Jean wasn't annoyed by her tail being stroked
- Whoever was ticked off about their ear being touched broke either the TV remote or a water jug
- The hissing cat either broke the TV remote or objected to being pet on the nose – but not both

- The claw-swiping kitty either destroyed the feather cushion in response to petting, or was Amanda – but not both

		Body part			Object			Response		
		Ear	Nose	Tail	Feather cushion	TV remote	Water jug	Biting	Hissing	Swiping claws
Cat	Amanda									
	Billie Jean									
	Dame Delilah									
Response	Biting									
	Hissing									
	Swiping claws									
Object	Feather cushion									
	TV remote									
	Water jug									

Cat	Body part	Response	Object

28. Hydration Havoc

Shannon, Chucky and Signora la Floof have all just made an exciting discovery: the water dispensers on their owners' fridges are motion-activated. Naturally, all three cats have spent a delightful afternoon flooding their respective kitchens, revelling in the wonders of gravity, science and plausible deniability. When their owners subsequently tried to create a physical barrier to prevent any further watery mishaps, the cats simply removed the obstacles and deposited them in a different room, ready to cause chaos once more.

Work out what each cat dispensed all over the floor, how their owner tried to block the flow, and where that physical obstacle ended up. **The cat who disposed of the large sponge also tore it to pieces, for a laugh. Who was it?**

- Shannon had not dispensed water
- The object which had been used to block ice cubes did not end up in the utility room
- The large sponge was used to block something other than ice cubes
- Shannon's efforts were either blocked with a large sponge or with sticky tape
- The water flow was not blocked with kitchen foil
- Signora La Floof was not the cat who spread ice cubes far and wide

- The large sponge ended up in the garage, but it was not the vehicle for the water spillage

		Dispensed item			Room			Barrier		
		Crushed ice	Ice cubes	Water	Bedroom	Garage	Utility room	Kitchen foil	Large sponge	Sticky tape
Cat	Chucky									
	Shannon									
	Signora la Floof									
Barrier	Kitchen foil									
	Large sponge									
	Sticky tape									
Room	Bedroom									
	Garage									
	Utility room									

Cat	Dispensed item	Barrier	Room

29. House Proud

Madeleine, Chicago and Edgar Allan Paw are house cats who love home and don't need to be anywhere else, thank you very much. Their owners, however, are senselessly obsessed with their feline well-being and have dragged the cats without consent to vets, where each will have a minor injury looked at. All three cats were transported with their favourite snuggly blankets (immediately ripped to pieces, as an act of protest), and they wasted no time in revealing their feelings when finally face-to-face with a vet.

Work out which cat had injured what body part, how many pieces they tore their favourite blanket into, and how they responded to the vet upon meeting them. **The cat who scratched the vet had ironically scratched themselves in the first place, resulting in the vet visit. Who was it?**

- Madeleine did not scratch the vet
- The cat who tore their blanket into four pieces was not the one who headbutted the vet
- Whoever injured their ear also scratched the vet
- Chicago threw up on the vet
- The cat with an injured front paw ripped their blanket into four pieces
- The headbutter ripped their blanket into more than two pieces

		Injured area			Response to vet			Blanket pieces		
		Belly	Ear	Front paw	Headbutted	Scratched	Threw up on	2	4	6
Cat	Chicago									
	Edgar Allan Paw									
	Madeleine									
Blanket pieces	2									
	4									
	6									
Response to vet	Headbutted									
	Scratched									
	Threw up on									

Cat	Injured area	Blanket pieces	Response to vet

30. Water'll You Do?

Sorcha, Hebe and Maestro Max have all just tripped over their own water bowls, despite the bowls being brightly coloured and also being located in the exact same spot for several years. The cats' initial responses to the spillages were distinct, but the optimistic trio soon saw an opportunity for playtime. Some might say that the cats each playing in the large puddles of water for several minutes was 'enterprising' and 'making the best of a bad situation', though, for some reason, their owners didn't.

Work out which cat tipped over what water bowl, how they initially felt about it, and for how long they subsequently played in the puddle. **The cat who played for the longest would tip their bowl over quite deliberately the next day to repeat the fun. Who was it?**

- Sorcha played in her puddle for exactly ten minutes
- The contents of the green bowl were played with for fifteen minutes
- The shocked cat either tipped over an orange bowl or played for fifteen minutes – but not both
- The shocked cat didn't play with the water for exactly ten minutes
- The cat who knocked over the green bowl was either distressed or played for exactly ten minutes – but not both

- Hebe was not the cat who played for fifteen minutes

		Colour			Play duration			Emotion		
		Green	Orange	Yellow	5 minutes	10 minutes	15 minutes	Amusement	Distress	Shock
Cat	Hebe									
	Maestro Max									
	Sorcha									
Emotion	Amusement									
	Distress									
	Shock									
Play duration	5 minutes									
	10 minutes									
	15 minutes									

Cat	Colour	Emotion	Play duration

31. Clean Sweep

Blossom, Ripley and The Prince of Darkness are cantankerous cats who don't like to confine their playtime in the house to daylight hours. Tonight's entertainment has somehow resulted in three different shower curtains being pulled down at various points during the night, ensuring a discombobulating wake-up call for their human housemates. The cats also knocked over an additional object in the ensuing fuss, just to make sure that absolutely nobody slept through it.

Work out which cat pulled down which shower curtain at what hour of the night, and what noisy object they knocked over shortly after. **The cat who knocked over the shampoo bottle also somehow managed to turn on the shower hose and drench themselves in the process. Who was it?**

- Blossom did not commit her crime at 1am
- The curtain pulled down at midnight was not the one adorned with lemons
- The sun-festooned curtain was either pulled down by Blossom or by The Prince of Darkness
- The Prince of Darkness did not attack the lemon-printed curtain
- Whoever brought down the lemon curtain, however, took down a shampoo bottle with it
- The Prince of Darkness did not act at midnight

- Ripley either pulled down the curtain emblazoned with waves or knocked over the shower radio – but not both

		Pattern			Object			Time of night		
		Lemons	Suns	Waves	Nail brush	Radio	Shampoo bottle	Midnight	1am	3am
Cat	Blossom									
	Ripley									
	The Prince of Darkness									
Time of night	Midnight									
	1am									
	3am									
Object	Nail brush									
	Radio									
	Shampoo bottle									

Cat	Pattern	Time of night	Object

32. Merry Mischief

Carol, Isambard and Mysterious Clive have all been getting into the festive spirit by destroying their owners' beloved Christmas ornaments mere moments after their owners have decorated. With astonishing speed, the cats have each smashed one bauble and pulled on a long string of tinsel, then ended on a high by eating the real berries from the wreaths their owners had just put the finishing touches to. All of the cats will now be taken to the vet, where they will all act extremely innocently despite comfortably ruining the first day of December.

Work out which cat smashed what bauble, pulled at which tinsel, and ate which berries. **The cat who ate the ivy berries then cheerfully vomited them up onto a pile of recently wrapped gifts. Who was it?**

- Carol did not smash the blue bauble
- Whoever pulled the silver tinsel also ate the holly berries
- The white tinsel was neither pulled by Carol nor smashed alongside the blue bauble
- Mysterious Clive was not the breaker of the green bauble
- Whoever ate the mistletoe berries had not just smashed the green bauble
- Isambard ate the holly berries with alarming speed

		Bauble colour			Berries			Tinsel colour		
		Blue	Green	Pink	Holly	Ivy	Mistletoe	Gold	Silver	White
Cat	Carol									
	Isambard									
	Mysterious Clive									
Tinsel colour	Gold									
	Silver									
	White									
Berries	Holly									
	Ivy									
	Mistletoe									

Cat	Bauble colour	Tinsel colour	Berries

33. Catch Me If You Can

Callum, Santiago and Lawless Larry are beholden to no one, and fear nothing. In an effort to assert their dominance, they have spent the afternoon relentlessly chasing and harassing three local dogs, whose only crime seems to have been their existence. The three cats have all been reprimanded by the owners of the pampered pooches, but their attitudes are not even remotely remorseful. In fact, they all seem rather proud of themselves.

Work out which cat chased which dog – both their name and appearance – and what their subsequent attitude showed. **The cat who chased the brown dog even managed to spook another cat in the process. Who was it?**

- Santiago was not the cat feeling smug
- Rory was not chased by a hubristic cat
- Max was either a golden-coated dog or was being chased by a smug cat – but not both
- Spike was either brown-coated or being chased by Lawless Larry – but not both
- The golden pooch was either being chased by Lawless Larry or by a smug cat – but not both
- Callum had either chased a black dog or was feeling hubristic – but not both
- Spike wasn't being chased by a hubristic cat

		Dog name			Attitude			Dog colour		
		Max	Rory	Spike	Hubristic	Imperious	Smug	Black	Brown	Gold
Cat	Callum									
	Lawless Larry									
	Santiago									
Dog colour	Black									
	Brown									
	Gold									
Attitude	Hubristic									
	Imperious									
	Smug									

Cat	Dog name	Dog colour	Attitude

34. Good Morning

Olive, Isa and Mrs Snuggleton are peaceful, snoozy kitties who enjoy a zen cat nap with their owners. They also enjoy asserting dominance, and today they have signalled the end of nap time by swiping the items on a nearby bedside table directly onto the floor with a clatter. Three books were swiped, then immediately drenched by three different glasses of liquid. The cats were most keen to make sure their drowsy owners met their immediate demands, which were all urgent matters definitely worth waking them up for.

Work out which cat swiped what book and which liquid, and what they wanted from their owner. **The cat who demanded attention would, in fact, run far away as soon as it was administered. Who was it?**

- The cat who wanted food was not the one who swiped a glass of water
- The purple book did not have water spilled on it
- The cat yowling for food was not the one who spilled the juice
- The cup of tea was either swiped by Mrs Snuggleton or onto a green book – but not both
- Isa swiped a glass of water with careful attention
- The tea was either swiped onto a green book or was spilled to demand food – but not both

- The green book was not the one covered in water
- Isa had not been the cat to demand freedom

		Book cover			Demand			Liquid		
		Green	Purple	Red	Attention	Food	Freedom	Juice	Tea	Water
Cat	Isa									
	Mrs Snuggleton									
	Olive									
Liquid	Juice									
	Tea									
	Water									
Demand	Attention									
	Food									
	Freedom									

Cat	Book cover	Liquid	Demand

35. Making a Splash

Eugene, Keanu and The Amazing Abigail suffer from serious fear of missing out, and today have decided to supervise their owners who are trying to take a nice hot bath in peace. Their human friends have all added something to the hot water which has given off an enticing smell, distracting the cats and causing them to fall into the suds. Not content with scratching their blameless owners in response, they also managed to swipe an additional dangerous item into the water with them. Ahh, so zen.

Work out which cat was enticed by which scent, what bath product had caused it, and what they accidentally brought into the bath with them. **The cat who swiped the razor into the bath will engage in a litter protest when they are finally dry. Who was it?**

- The bubbles were lavender-scented
- The medicine was either brought in by The Amazing Abigail or by the cat who sought out the lavender aroma – but not both
- The razor was not swiped by The Amazing Abigail
- The Amazing Abigail hadn't been tempted by the smell of ginger
- The candle did not fall into the bath adorned with bath salts
- Eugene did not bring the medicine into the mix

- The cat who was lured in by the bath salts was either Eugene or the cat who brought in the razor – but not both

		Scent			Dangerous item			Addition		
		Coconut	Ginger	Lavender	Candle	Medicine	Razor	Bath bomb	Bath salts	Bubbles
Cat	Eugene									
	Keanu									
	The Amazing Abigail									
Addition	Bath bomb									
	Bath salts									
	Bubbles									
Dangerous item	Candle									
	Medicine									
	Razor									

Cat	Scent	Addition	Dangerous item

36. Blind Spots

Magdalena, Phoenix and Malcolm the Majestic are inquisitive cats who like to find out all they can about the known universe. In the middle of the night, therefore, they have all jumped up onto the blinds in their owners' homes to get a better look at a sparkly object they have observed outside. Because the blinds were not designed to support the weight of cats, destructive pandemonium was the result, with every cohabiting human woken up by the ensuing rumpus. All in the name of science, of course.

Work out which cat jumped onto what blind, what they tried to observe, and how many people they woke. **The cat who wanted to look at the street light had, in fact, seen that same street light every day for the last decade. Who was it?**

- The cat who woke up exactly one person had been entranced by an aeroplane
- The street-light-obsessed cat was not the one who woke up five people
- The cat who did wake up five people was either Malcolm the Majestic or the cat who became entangled in a wooden blind – but not both
- Magdalena was either caught up in a cloth blind or woke five people – but not both
- The cloth-bound cat did manage to wake up exactly three people

- Malcolm the Majestic woke up more than one person – but was not the cat caught up in the cloth blind

		Blind material			People woken			Sparkly object		
		Cloth	Metal	Wood	1	3	5	Aeroplane	Moon	Street light
Cat	Magdalena									
	Malcolm the Majestic									
	Phoenix									
Sparkly object	Aeroplane									
	Moon									
	Street light									
People woken	1									
	3									
	5									

Cat	Blind material	Sparkly object	People woken

37. Service Charge

Cosima, Evander and Princess Peach have spent a cosy afternoon watching their owners standing over a hot stove and cooking up a delicious supper. At the moment of transfer to the dining table, however, all three cats tripped up their owners with what can only be described as perfect timing, resulting in the dishes going flying. Although only one of the cats acted out of pure spite, all three have been banished from the kitchen forthwith, with not even so much as a catnip for the road.

Work out which cat tripped up a chef carrying what dish, why they did so, and where they were banished. **The cat who acted out of spite managed to snaffle some spilled food from the floor before their exile. Who was it?**

- Evander was not the cat banished outside
- The cat who acted out of curiosity was either banished to the living room or had sent a casserole flying – but not both
- Evander was not the cause of the soup spillage, and neither was Cosima
- Whoever caused the soup spillage was not sent outside for it
- The soup was spilled purely as an act of curiosity
- Evander had either acted out of spite or was exiled to the living room – but not both

- The casserole disaster was not borne out of clumsiness

		Dish			Banished to			Reason		
		Casserole	Soup	Spaghetti	Hallway	Living room	Outside	Clumsiness	Curiosity	Spite
Cat	Cosima									
	Evander									
	Princess Peach									
Reason	Clumsiness									
	Curiosity									
	Spite									
Banished to	Hallway									
	Living room									
	Outside									

Cat	Dish	Reason	Banished to

38. Not Very Smart Casual

Sophie, Bubbles and Calamity Jane each have beautiful fur coats, and don't understand their owners' constant need to wear new clothing every day. Their blatant disrespect for fashion has been demonstrated overnight, since all three cats have attacked a high-quality item of clothing that their owner had left out to wear the next day. While the items of clothing are all different in terms of fabric and colour, the cats are all equally proud of their destructive efforts – and in equal amounts of trouble.

Work out which cat attacked which item, what material it consisted of, and what colour it was. **The cat who destroyed the linen item also sank their teeth into a new pair of shoes for good measure. Who was it?**

- Bubbles cheerfully destroyed a mauve garment
- The coat was not mustard in colour
- Calamity Jane was not the destroyer of the wool item
- The cotton garment was not mauve in colour
- Calamity Jane did not destroy a shirt, though she did destroy something mustard-toned
- The trousers were not made of cotton
- Sophie had either destroyed a shirt or trousers

		Item			Colour			Material		
		Coat	Shirt	Trousers	Mauve	Mulberry	Mustard	Cotton	Linen	Wool
Cat	Bubbles									
	Calamity Jane									
	Sophie									
Material	Cotton									
	Linen									
	Wool									
Colour	Mauve									
	Mulberry									
	Mustard									

Cat	Item	Material	Colour

39. A Little Tied Up

JackJack, Mystique and Lois Lane are scientists, and also agents of chaos. Today, they have explored both of these aspects of their personalities by tangling up the cables belonging to three different household items, and leaving them in such a state that their owners will have to spend several minutes disentangling them. The cats, however, will be nowhere to be found during the great disentangling – they will, instead, be starting their next experiment, to find out how many live mice they can sneak into the house before anybody notices.

Work out which cat tangled up what colour cable, which device it was for, and how long it took someone to untangle it. **The cat whose owner took the longest to untangle the cables will later bring in four live mice. Who was it?**

- The silver cables were for the vacuum cleaner – but they were not the ones which took 45 minutes to untangle
- Lois Lane's efforts did not take exactly 30 minutes to untangle
- JackJack was not the tangler of the red cables
- The cables which took exactly 30 minutes to untangle were for the TV
- The heater cables were either tangled up by Mystique or by JackJack

- Mystique's entanglement was not the one which took exactly 30 minutes to untangle

		Cable colour			Untangling time			Device		
		Black	Red	Silver	20 mins	30 mins	45 mins	Heater	TV	Vacuum cleaner
Cat	JackJack									
	Lois Lane									
	Mystique									
Device	Heater									
	TV									
	Vacuum cleaner									
Untangling time	20 mins									
	30 mins									
	45 mins									

Cat	Cable colour	Device	Untangling time

40. Cut to the Chase

Sydney, Royce and Simon the Stripey are certified lone rangers, who don't like anyone stepping into their territory. Three local cats didn't get the memo, however, and have accidentally crossed paths with the mean-spirited moggies. The three victims offended the original cats in various different ways, though all three were subsequently chased through a number of nearby gardens until the threat was deemed to have been neutralised.

Work out which cat chased which victim, what their victim had done to offend them, and how many gardens they chased them through. **The cat who pounced on their suspect, merely for existing, is a known menace from whom even some human neighbours steer clear. Who was it?**

- Royce did not run through seven gardens, and was not offended by another cat existing
- The cat chased through exactly four gardens was either accused of staring or was chased by Simon the Stripey – but not both
- Pom Pom was not the cat chased through exactly five gardens
- The punishment for trespassing involved being chased through fewer than seven gardens
- Melon had not been perceived to be trespassing
- Pom Pom was not the cat whose mere existence caused a stir

- The cat chased through exactly five gardens was either chased by Sydney or was in trouble for merely existing – but not both

		Victim cat			Gardens chased through			Perceived offence		
		Loopy	Melon	Pom Pom	4	5	7	Existing	Staring	Trespassing
Cat	Royce									
	Simon the Stripey									
	Sydney									
Perceived offence	Existing									
	Staring									
	Trespassing									
Gardens chased through	4									
	5									
	7									

Cat	Victim cat	Perceived offence	Gardens chased through

41. Waste Not Want Not

Llewellyn, Crusoe and Mike the Magician are resourceful cats, who strongly believe in reducing household waste. Unfortunately for their owners, they tend to demonstrate this by retrieving items of rubbish which have already been thrown away and distributing them around the house at random. Today has been no exception, though the cats have thoughtfully let their owners know about the schemes in their own ways.

Work out which cat pulled what item from the trash, where they deposited it, and how they notified their owners. **The cat who picked out the used diaper will be banned from the house for the night. Who was it?**

- The banana peel was either left by Crusoe or by a cat who subsequently meowed – but not both
- Crusoe didn't place his item on the front doormat, and luckily nor was that the location of the used diaper
- Purring did not accompany the deposit of an item in the toilet bowl
- Whoever had redistributed the used diaper was not screaming about it
- The banana peel was either pulled out by a meowing cat, or by Llewellyn – but not both
- Llewellyn wasn't screaming, anyway

		Item			Noti-fication			Location		
		Banana peel	Used diaper	Yoghurt pot	Meowing	Purring	Screaming	Front doormat	Kitchen table	Toilet bowl
Cat	Crusoe									
	Llewellyn									
	Mike the Magician									
Location	Front doormat									
	Kitchen table									
	Toilet bowl									
Noti-fication	Meowing									
	Purring									
	Screaming									

Cat	Item	Location	Notification

42. A Bundle of Joy

Maia, Lancelot and Jane Pawsten are all obliged to visit the local vet, and are all extremely unhappy about it. Their owners have tried to pacify them by including their favourite toys in their carrying crates, but the cats still took several vicious swipes at their human captors which may require additional medical intervention later on. The recalcitrant cats do seem to be experiencing some variation in their emotions, though all of them would probably identify 'hatred' very near the top of the list.

Work out which cat took which number of swipes, what toy they were pacified with, and what their chief emotion was. **The cat who took the greatest number of swipes threw in a few hisses, to really get the point across. Who was it?**

- Lancelot was experiencing feelings of revulsion
- The fluffy bunny was not the toy belonging to the cat who took a total of twelve swipes
- Whoever was supposedly being pacified with the feather duster was responding with abhorrence
- Maia was given a fluffy bunny as a consolation prize
- The squeaky mouse was not the toy offered to the cat who took the greatest number of swipes
- Lancelot was not the cat who swiped exactly nine times

		Number of swipes			Chief emotion			Toy		
		5	9	12	Abhorrence	Loathing	Revulsion	Feather duster	Fluffy bunny	Squeaky mouse
Cat	Jane Pawsten									
	Lancelot									
	Maia									
Toy	Feather duster									
	Fluffy bunny									
	Squeaky mouse									
Chief emotion	Abhorrence									
	Loathing									
	Revulsion									

Cat	Number of swipes	Toy	Chief emotion

43. Sleepwalkers

Maurice, Sirius and The Lion King are not known for their subtlety, and tonight they have chosen to communicate with their owners in the best way they know: by walking across their faces while they are sleeping. The three cats prowled at different times of the night and they each had their own reasons for the interruption, ranging from sweet to sociopathic. All three cats were thence banished from their owners' sleeping quarters, but that merely gave them more time to plot out their next act of chaos.

Work out which cat walked on their owner's face at what time, their reason for doing so, and the length of their resulting banishment. **The cat who was sentenced to the longest banishment will actually hide under the bed in two days' time to circumvent the ruling. Who was it?**

- The cat who acted at 3am was not the one subsequently banished for four days
- The cat who acted on feelings of ennui was not the one who was punished for exactly six days
- Sirius acted at 3am, but not out of ennui
- The cat banished for six days had appeared at 5am
- The cat acting out of loneliness was not the one who was banished for the longest time
- Maurice did not commit his crime at 5am

		Time			Days banished			Motive		
		1am	3am	5am	4 days	6 days	8 days	Caprice	Ennui	Loneliness
Cat	Maurice									
	Sirius									
	The Lion King									
Motive	Caprice									
	Ennui									
	Loneliness									
Days banished	4 days									
	6 days									
	8 days									

Cat	Time	Motive	Days banished

44. Pot Luck

Fleur, Kylo and Little Miss Fluff would have perfect lives if they didn't have to share their homes with a completely ridiculous canine companion. The three cats are pampered beyond belief, but years after being joined by a dog in the home they are still expressing their displeasure in the pettiest ways they can. This evening they have opted to eat the dogs' dinners as well as their own, ensuring that the pups go hungry for the night and that dominance is fully asserted once more.

Work out what each cat was offered for their own supper, what they stole from the family dog instead, and what each maligned dog's name is. **The cat who stole Barry's dinner also left a dead mouse in his bed, for good measure. Who was it?**

- Barry had either been given beef or had his dinner stolen by Kylo – but not both
- Little Miss Fluff had not been served prawns
- Mackerel was either the supper offered to Barry's antagonizer or to Little Miss Fluff – but not both
- Whoever had originally been given prawns either snaffled some turkey or snaffled some of Barry's dinner – but not both
- The tuna supper wasn't followed by a beef course
- Clive's dinner was stolen by Kylo

		Cat's supper			Dog's name			Dog's supper		
		Mackerel	Prawns	Tuna	Barry	Clive	Maureen	Beef	Pork	Turkey
Cat	Fleur									
	Kylo									
	Little Miss Fluff									
Dog's supper	Beef									
	Pork									
	Turkey									
Dog's name	Barry									
	Clive									
	Maureen									

Cat	Cat's supper	Dog's supper	Dog's name

45. A Choir of Anarchists

Ezra, Griffin and Major Mischief are music-makers, who express their feelings through the medium of song. Unfortunately for their owners, the only song they know is one of incessant yowling – and it is often launched into at inappropriate moments. The cats have just interrupted three important phone calls with songs expressing different emotions, all lasting for different amounts of time – and all of which felt like an eternity to their owners.

Work out which cat was feeling which emotion, what phone call they interrupted, and for how long their yowling continued. **The cat who interrupted the job interview also took a few swipes at the phone, for fun. Who was it?**

- Petulance was either Ezra's emotion or felt by the cat interrupting the credit-card call – but not both
- The cat who yowled for exactly three minutes successfully sabotaged a job interview
- Major Mischief was not feeling existential dread
- The petulant cat was not the one who yowled for eight minutes straight
- The mortgage application call was ruined by a yowl lasting exactly four minutes – but this musician was not yowling out of petulance
- Major Mischief did not ruin the mortgage application

		Feeling			Time			Call		
		Cantankerousness	Existential dread	Petulance	3 minutes	4 minutes	8 minutes	Credit card company	Job interview	Mortgage application
Cat	Ezra									
	Griffin									
	Major Mischief									
Call	Credit card company									
	Job interview									
	Mortgage application									
Time	3 minutes									
	4 minutes									
	8 minutes									

Cat	Feeling	Call	Time

Chapter 3

Perplexing Pusses

46. A Little Birdie

Paloma, Titus, Serena and Sandy Claws have each brought a bird home and displayed it on their owner's pillow with great pride. Strangely, the human recipients don't seem to be grateful for their gifts, which the cats all took the trouble to decapitate before presenting to them. Inexplicably banished, each cat has slunk off to a hiding spot in their house to spook their owner, and plot their revenge.

Work out which cat brought in which bird, and where they subsequently hid after being banished. **The cat who escaped to the pantry would later be discovered feasting upon a forbidden wheel of cheese. Who was it?**

- The wren was either brought in by Titus or the cat hiding in the downstairs toilet – but not both
- The shoe cupboard was not the hiding place of Sandy Claws
- Either Titus brought in the wren, or the wren-bringer hid in the shoe cupboard – but not both
- The cat who caught a tit hid neither in the downstairs toilet nor the shoe cupboard
- Either way, whoever hid in the shoe cupboard hadn't brought in a robin
- Serena was not the cat hiding in the pantry
- Titus hid in the porch

- The shoe cupboard was the hiding place of either Serena or the cat who brought in the magpie – but not both

		Bird				Hiding place			
		Magpie	Robin	Tit	Wren	Downstairs toilet	Pantry	Porch	Shoe cupboard
Cat	Paloma								
	Sandy Claws								
	Serena								
	Titus								
Hiding place	Downstairs toilet								
	Pantry								
	Porch								
	Shoe cupboard								

Cat	Bird	Hiding place

47. Love Hurts

Calvin, Daisy, Halo and Officer Snuggles love their owners unconditionally, and express their love for them every day in different ways. Today's method has involved sinking their sharp teeth into one of their owner's body parts with absolutely no warning whatsoever, resulting in a speedy trip to a medical facility for sterile dressings. The cats each had different reasons for their surprise attacks, although the owners seem to be uniformly unhappy about them.

Work out which cat bit which body part, and why.

The cat whose motive was affection actually managed to cause the greatest injury. Who was it?

- Calvin was not the toe-biter
- The knee was either bitten by Officer Snuggles or by Halo
- Calvin acted out of malice (and made no apology for it)
- Halo acted out of open hostility (and again, did not care)
- The knee-biter acted with (supposed) affection
- Halo did not bite anyone's toes
- Calvin did not bite anyone's nose

		Body part				Reason			
		Hand	Knee	Nose	Toe	Affection	Hostility	Inquisitiveness	Malice
Cat	Calvin								
	Daisy								
	Halo								
	Officer Snuggles								
Reason	Affection								
	Hostility								
	Inquisitiveness								
	Malice								

Cat	Body part	Reason

48. Food for Thought

Drew, Earl, Neptune and The Void are always extremely well-fed cats, but that doesn't stop them screaming for more food as soon as their bowls are empty. The four cats have all demanded a second helping of their supper, mainly through the medium of headbutts and yowls. When their second course was administered, however, the cats had the audacity to pretend they'd never even requested it in the first place – which is all part of the fun.

Work out which cat demanded more of what food, and their response when their wishes were finally granted.

The cat who walked away will continue their yowling in a different room, for secret reasons. Who was it?

- Drew had either been given sardines or responded with slow blinking – but not both
- The cat who walked away had been given duck
- The Void was not screaming, and neither was Neptune
- Drew was not the cat who demanded more chicken
- The Void had requested more sardines

		Food demanded				Response			
		Chicken	Cod	Duck	Sardines	Biting ankles	Screaming	Slow blinking	Walking away
Cat	Drew								
	Earl								
	Neptune								
	The Void								
Response	Biting ankles								
	Screaming								
	Slow blinking								
	Walking away								

Cat	Food demanded	Response

49. Sneaky Beasts

Agnes, Catriona, Saint and The Escape Artist have all been headbutting their owners for the last five minutes or so, but refuse to reveal their motives. The capricious kitties each have their own reasons for the incessant nudging, but it's far more entertaining if they let their owners guess. All of the guesses are incorrect, of course: the cats are just trying to distract their owners from a totally different, secret crime they have recently committed. Genius.

Work out which cat was thought to be headbutting for which reason, and what their true secret crime was.

The cat who unravelled the jumper hid their evidence under the sofa, and won't be rumbled for weeks. Who was it?

- The Escape Artist's actions were chalked up to love
- Saint destroyed a toilet roll
- Catriona chewed a shoe
- The cat who brought in a mouse has fooled their owners into thinking that the headbutting is merely for entertainment
- Saint was not thought to be headbutting out of friendship

		Guessed reason				Secret crime			
		Entertainment	Friendship	Incorrigibility	Love	Brought in mouse	Chewed shoe	Destroyed toilet roll	Unravelled jumper
Cat	Agnes								
	Catriona								
	Saint								
	The Escape Artist								
Secret crime	Brought in mouse								
	Chewed shoe								
	Destroyed toilet roll								
	Unravelled jumper								

Cat	Guessed reason	Secret crime

50. Selective Fun

Jacqueline, Lennox, Achilles and The Mousetrap are playful purrers, but prefer to have fun on their own terms. As such, they have studiously ignored the brand-new cat toy that their owner has just unboxed for them, and, instead, have run into another room to select a new toy for themselves from a list of items which are strictly off-limits. The cats will eventually play with their designated new toys – but only when they can be sure their owners aren't looking.

Work out which cat ignored which toy, and what they played with instead.

The cat who pulled apart a throw cushion succeeded in spreading feathers absolutely everywhere. Who was it?

- Achilles played with an unauthorized toothbrush
- Lennox had not been given a rubber fish
- Jacqueline was not the destroyer of the throw cushion
- The scratching post was studiously ignored by Achilles
- Jacqueline feigned indifference to her personal yurt
- The salt shaker was played with by either Lennox or Achilles

		Toy ignored				Preferred object			
		Ball with bell	Personal yurt	Rubber fish	Scratching post	Mop head	Salt shaker	Throw cushion	Toothbrush
Cat	Achilles								
	Jacqueline								
	Lennox								
	The Mousetrap								
Preferred object	Mop head								
	Salt shaker								
	Throw cushion								
	Toothbrush								

Cat	Toy ignored	Preferred object

51. High Flyers

Dylan, Jeffery, Callisto and Shambolic Steve are on a high – a literal one. All four cats have climbed onto the roofs of their houses and have been yowling for several hours to indicate that they are stuck and require rescuing. The cats had different reasons for venturing up high, though they all have fearlessness in common. When the cats are finally rescued, they will, of course, hop down without a fuss, having been able to rescue themselves all along – but where's the fun in that?

Work out why each cat climbed on the roof, and the length of time they were each 'stuck' there. **The cat who hopped up for a bit of sunbathing will cheerfully hiss at their rescuer, just to wind them up. Who was it?**

- The sunbathing cat was 'stuck' the longest time, but this wasn't Callisto
- Shambolic Steve was 'stuck' for either 3 hours or 6 hours
- Callisto was not the cat 'stuck' for either two hours or five hours
- The cat who was 'stuck' for exactly five hours hadn't gone to seek better views
- Dylan wasn't the cat who ended up on the roof thanks to a lack of attention
- The three-hour stint was endured by a cat stalking birds

		Reason				Time on roof			
		Better view	Not paying attention	Stalking bird	Sunbathing	2 hours	3 hours	5 hours	6 hours
Cat	Callisto								
	Dylan								
	Jeffery								
	Shambolic Steve								
Time on roof	2 hours								
	3 hours								
	5 hours								
	6 hours								

Cat	Reason	Time on roof

52. The Lived-In Look

Finn, Jennifer, Troy and The Boss are benevolent rulers who generally allow their owners to enjoy their shared homes in peace. Today, however, the humans have each brought home a new piece of furniture, which the cats were not made aware of in advance. All four pieces are now sporting a 'shabby-chic' look, after the cats have sunk their claws into them and scratched at the surfaces. Their motives were all subtly different, but the destruction is quite uniform.

Work out which cat scratched which piece of furniture, and why.

The cat who took offence at the armchair will later refuse to let anyone else sit in it. Who was it?

- The laundry basket was either damaged by The Boss or the cat that was feeling vindictive – but not both
- The Boss acted out of listlessness
- Jennifer was not the vindictive cat
- The nightstand was damaged either by Troy or by The Boss
- The armchair was damaged out of vindictiveness
- The cat acting out of experimentation was either offended by the footstool or the laundry basket

		Furniture				Motive			
		Armchair	Footstool	Laundry basket	Nightstand	Experimentation	Listlessness	Research	Vindictiveness
Cat	Finn								
	Jennifer								
	The Boss								
	Troy								
Motive	Experimentation								
	Listlessness								
	Research								
	Vindictiveness								

Cat	Furniture	Motive

53. Apology Not Accepted

Evan, Jericho, Nero and Prue the Prancer are bundles of fun, day and night. On this particular night they have all woken up their owners in different ways, but all at the stroke of midnight. The cats quickly gathered that their actions were unpopular, and thus set about bringing their beloved humans a gift to apologise, which was thoughtful. Unfortunately for the owners it was also nightmarish, because all of the apology gifts were live animals.

Work out which cat woke up their owner in which way, and what they brought them as an apology. **The cat who brought in a live vole then proceeded to play with it for half an hour. Who was it?**

- Jericho did not bring in a toad
- The rat was not brought in by Nero
- Prue the Prancer brought in a (noisy) grasshopper
- The water glass had been smashed either by Evan or by Jericho
- Prue the Prancer hadn't sat on her owner's face (on this particular occasion)
- Whoever brought in the live vole had already woken up their owner with ceaseless screaming
- Evan had either smashed the water glass or brought in a live rat – but not both

		Method				Animal			
		Ceaseless screaming	Setting off alarm	Sitting on face	Smashing water glass	Grasshopper	Rat	Toad	Vole
Cat	Evan								
	Jericho								
	Nero								
	Prue the Prancer								
Animal	Grasshopper								
	Rat								
	Toad								
	Vole								

Cat	Method	Animal

54. Public Enemies

Chelsea, Jade, Andromeda and Captain Chaos are spirited cats who have been kept indoors this week, after several reported incidents with other local kitties. Their spirit of chaos knows no bounds, however, and somehow the four felonious felines have managed to escape their indoor prisons to wreak havoc on the outside world. The four cats each have different activities planned during their jailbreaks, though all of them will return in an hour with a very smug attitude indeed.

Work out which cat was planning to engage in which activity, and what attitude they each came back with. **The cat who planned to terrorize neighbours briefly broke into someone else's house in the process. Who was it?**

- The cat who planned to terrorize neighbours didn't come back with a flippant attitude
- Captain Chaos did not plan to inspire fear or to terrorize neighbours
- Jade wasn't showing off an aura of jauntiness when she returned
- Andromeda was indifferent when she returned
- The cat who planned to make enemies returned looking indifferent
- The cat who went out to inspire fear was full of nonchalance later

		Planned activity				Attitude			
		Being a menace	Inspiring fear	Making enemies	Terrorizing neighbours	Flippancy	Indifference	Jauntiness	Nonchalance
Cat	Andromeda								
	Captain Chaos								
	Chelsea								
	Jade								
Attitude	Flippancy								
	Indifference								
	Jauntiness								
	Nonchalance								

Cat	Planned activity	Attitude

55. On Your Own Terms

Edgar, Jolene, Ajax and Emma the Brave like to play hard to get, and sometimes in a very literal sense. These aloof cats have been studiously ignoring their owners' repeated calls, despite their human friends using the cats' very favourite words to try and entice them. Despite their standoffishness, the cats will later appear at a time that suits them and demand that their owners indulge their requests, timing it to perfectly coincide with a task which can only be interrupted with great inconvenience.

Work out which cat ignored which word, and what they later came in to demand.

The cat who demanded food would, in fact, wander off as soon as their supper was served. Who was it?

- Whoever wanted cuddles had studiously ignored the word 'dindins' earlier
- Edgar did not demand either food or grooming
- The word 'treat' was ignored either by Ajax or by Emma the Brave
- The cat whose favourite word was 'fluffy' later demanded grooming
- Emma the Brave sought out cuddles

		Favourite word: Bedtime	Favourite word: Dindins	Favourite word: Fluffy	Favourite word: Treat	Demand: Attention	Demand: Cuddles	Demand: Food	Demand: Grooming
Cat	Ajax								
	Edgar								
	Emma the Brave								
	Jolene								
Demand	Attention								
	Cuddles								
	Food								
	Grooming								

Cat	Favourite word	Demand

56. Temporary Release

Frances, Juniper, Dalloway and Chief Ratter have all interrupted their owners' important daytime activities with an urgent request of their own: to be let out into the great outdoors. The cats have mewled, meowed and straight-up screamed at their human friends for several minutes, though, of course, when the door was opened for them they simply retreated back into the house to commit dastardly crimes elsewhere.

Work out which cat interrupted which human activity, and what they slunk off to do when the door was opened. **The cat who interrupted a nap will do so again in precisely one hour, as a result of their future crime. Who was it?**

- Juniper scampered off to eat socks
- The litter protest followed either the work call or the laundry administration
- Chief Ratter interrupted a work call
- Dalloway did not get in the way of a nap
- The interrupted nap was not followed by the smashing of glasses
- Frances had not ruined laundry administration, and nor did she wander off to climb the curtains
- The interrupted laundry task was not followed up with a litter protest

		Activity interrupted				Secondary crime			
		Cleaning	Laundry administration	Nap	Work call	Climbing on curtains	Eating socks	Litter protest	Smashing glasses
Cat	Chief Ratter								
	Dalloway								
	Frances								
	Juniper								
Secondary crime	Climbing on curtains								
	Eating socks								
	Litter protest								
	Smashing glasses								

Cat	Activity interrupted	Secondary crime

57. Second Servings

Hilary, Jeepers, Aeneas and Colonel Mouser each have a refined culinary palate, and also a real penchant for mayhem. After watching their owners carefully prepare a meal for themselves, the cats have waited until the suppers have been plated up on the kitchen countertop to dramatically swipe the dishes to the floor. The food is, of course, ruined, and the plates it was served upon shattered into several pieces. The cats don't mind, because they have already eaten, and won't have to clean it up. Bon appetit.

Work out which cat swiped what food onto the floor, and which plate went with it. **The cat who swiped the glass plate will claim it was all in the name of science, but really they were just feeling vindictive. Who was it?**

- The glass plate either once bore lamb curry or was smashed by Colonel Mouser – but not both
- Hilary smashed a stoneware or a porcelain plate
- The china plate was not smashed by Jeepers
- The pasta bake had been on a porcelain plate
- The jacket potato had once been on a china plate
- Colonel Mouser hadn't ruined a jacket potato dinner
- The plate Colonel Mouser smashed was either made of porcelain or of china

		Food				Plate			
		Chicken bagel	Jacket potato	Lamb curry	Pasta bake	China	Glass	Porcelain	Stoneware
Cat	Aeneas								
	Colonel Mouser								
	Hilary								
	Jeepers								
Plate	China								
	Glass								
	Porcelain								
	Stoneware								

Cat	Food	Plate

58. Siren Song

Idina, Muriel, Neo and Ray the Rioter have been treating their owners to a chorus of incessant yowls for several minutes, without revealing their motives. Their harried owners have been left to guess at their poor kitties' predicaments, and have offered various treats and soothing words to try and calm the caterwaulers. The cats are, of course, absolutely fine – their true motives have nothing to do with personal disquiet whatsoever, but that's their secret to keep.

Work out which cat is perceived to be yowling for which reason, and what their actual reason is.

The cat whose true motive is tedium will pull the same stunt at 3am, though their owner will be much less sympathetic then. Who was it?

- Idina's owner thought she was yowling with distress
- The cat whose real motive was impishness was thought to be either hungry or lonely
- Devilment was initially misinterpreted as anxiety
- Ray the Rioter was not the cat thought to be hungry
- Muriel acted out of mischief, but was not thought to be hungry

		Perceived reason				Actual reason			
		Anxiety	Distress	Hunger	Loneliness	Devilment	Impishness	Mischief	Tedium
Cat	Idina								
	Muriel								
	Neo								
	Ray the Rioter								
Actual reason	Devilment								
	Impishness								
	Mischief								
	Tedium								

Cat	Perceived reason	Actual reason

59. Home from Home

Isaac, Opal, Lysander and Disgraceful Grace have been taken by the spirit of adventure, and specifically have taken themselves off into someone else's house on their street for an illegal homestay. Having snuck in through an unmanned entrance, the cats have then all settled down into a cosy hiding spot in their temporary accommodation, ready to jump out and cause maximum confusion and panic later on – their favourite holiday activity.

Work out which cat has broken into what house and where they chose to hide within it.

The cat who broke into number 11 will be horrified to later find out that another cat already lives there. Who was it?

- Isaac was not the cat hiding in the recycling bin, nor did he venture into the dog's bed
- Disgraceful Grace didn't break into number 13
- Whoever broke into house number 11 hid in their recycling bin
- Opal broke into number 25 and hid in the shoe rack
- The dog's bed was not in house number 4

		House number				Hiding place			
		4	11	13	25	Dog's bed	Kitchen table	Recycling bin	Shoe rack
Cat	Disgraceful Grace								
	Isaac								
	Lysander								
	Opal								
Hiding place	Dog's bed								
	Kitchen table								
	Recycling bin								
	Shoe rack								

Cat	House number	Hiding place

60. Yes, But Also No

Orla, Enya, Newton and Disorderly Derek love cuddles, attention, fuss and personal space. Their somewhat conflicting desires came into their own this morning when they demanded, by several means of communication, that their owners pet them, before quickly becoming enraged when their bewildered owners actually obliged. The cats have since slunk off into another room to be alone with their thoughts, though they will soon meow with loneliness once more.

Work out which cat communicated with what method, and which room they then snuck into. **The cat who snuck into the kitchen briefly entertained themselves by sticking their face in a glass of fruit juice. Who was it?**

- Whoever slunk off to the kitchen had started out by nudging their owner
- Enya slunk off to the living room
- The cat who had been chirping wasn't in the garage
- Newton had neither been whining nor chirping
- The garage was not the final location of the cat who had been staring intensely
- Disorderly Derek had chosen nudging as his main method of communication

		Communication method				Room			
		Chirping	Intense staring	Nudging	Whining	Bathroom	Garage	Kitchen	Living room
Cat	Disorderly Derek								
	Enya								
	Newton								
	Orla								
Room	Bathroom								
	Garage								
	Kitchen								
	Living room								

Cat	Communication method	Room

Chapter 4

Problematic Pusses

61. Going Nowhere Fast

Pamela, Orville, Paris and Empurror Julius have all been ordered into their carrying crates, and extraordinary protests have erupted. Despite their owners' good intentions for these departures from home, and their gentle bribery with the cats' favourite treats, it has taken a full hour to coax each kitty into their secure carrier.

The trouble has not ended there, however. Alongside a spot of hissing and spitting, the cats have used their time in solitary confinement not to come to terms with their own feelings, but instead to protest further, and plan out future vengeance. The cats will eventually emerge in a docile state, although they will simply want to lure their captors into a false sense of security before seeking retribution for this most unjust of imprisonments.

Work out which cat was being moved for which reason, what treat they were bribed with, and what they got up to while confined to their crates.

The cat who spent their time sulking has torn apart the blanket which was included in their cell, to really emphasise their displeasure. Who was it?

- The cat embroiled in a house move spent their time plotting
- Paris was either offered salmon or did some plotting – but not both
- Pamela was either plotting or being taken on vacation – but not both
- The trout was either offered to the cat moving house, or the one experiencing an emergency
- Catnip was either offered to Empurror Julius or the one who had been plotting – but not both
- Either way, the catnip was not the bribe offered to the howling cat
- The cat caught up in an emergency was either seething or called Pamela – but not both
- Paris was not on the way to the vet
- Empurror Julius was being taken on vacation

		Reason				Activity				Treat			
		Emergency	House move	Vacation	Vet visit	Howling	Plotting	Seething	Sulking	Catnip	Chicken	Salmon	Trout
Cat	Empurror Julius												
	Orville												
	Pamela												
	Paris												
Treat	Catnip												
	Chicken												
	Salmon												
	Trout												
Activity	Howling												
	Plotting												
	Seething												
	Sulking												

Cat	Reason	Treat	Activity

62. Not Sharing, Not Caring

Philomena, Reagan, Zenith and Inigo the Interrupter are used to ruling the proverbial roost, and have been therefore flabbergasted to find out that their owners have brought home a second cat. The new cats are shamelessly being shown much more attention by their traitorous human 'friends'. This disgraceful turn of events has absolutely nothing to do with the fact that all four original cats have spent their entire lives crafting aloof and standoffish personalities in the hopes that everyone will leave them alone.

The cats have not – yet – resorted to violence against their new roommates, but they have decided to first assert their dominance in the pettiest way they can think of: by refusing to share anything with them at all.

Work out how each cat felt about the new arrival, what the new arrival's name was, and what item they refused to share with them.

The cat who refused to share a water bowl with the new cat will simply tip it over whenever the other cat approaches, even if that means they both go thirsty for the day. Who was it?

- One of the cats was feeling resentful towards Scamp
- Either the water bowl was not being shared by Inigo, or was being kept away from Polka Dot – but not both
- The cat who wouldn't share a scratching post wasn't the one feeling affronted
- Reagan was neither feeling disgusted nor offended
- Neither the window-seat-hogger nor the litter-tray-dictator were offended
- Zenith was either bullying Jinx or not sharing a scratching post – but not both
- The litter tray was not the commodity denied to Polka Dot
- The scratching post was not the item controlled by Inigo the Interruptor, and nor was it Zenith's
- Philomena had been forced to cohabit with Scamp

		Attitude				Item				New cat			
		Affronted	Disgusted	Offended	Resentful	Litter tray	Scratching post	Water bowl	Window seat	Jinx	Mina	Polka Dot	Scamp
Cat	Inigo the Interrupter												
	Philomena												
	Reagan												
	Zenith												
New cat	Jinx												
	Mina												
	Polka Dot												
	Scamp												
Item	Litter tray												
	Scratching post												
	Water bowl												
	Window seat												

Cat	Attitude	New cat	Item

63. Night-Time Nuisance

Ralph, Cassini, Ulysses and Hairy Claire have all been sleeping soundly next to their snoozy owners, but they'd hate for anyone to be getting too comfortable. Having woken up from their slumber in the middle of the night, all four cats have turned their attention to mischief, and, in this case, the manifestation of that malignant mischief was the swiping of exactly one item from their owner's nightstand onto the floor.

Each item was selected to make the maximum amount of noise, and the swipes occurred at different times of the night – although none of them could be even vaguely considered a convenient time to wake up to a clatter. The cats all had their reasons for the unexpected chaos tonight, although they all generally suffer from an inescapable urge to cause mayhem.

Work out which cat swept which item onto the floor, what time they did it, and their reason for doing so.

The cat who acted purely out of love will be banished from the bedroom herewith, and be forced to plot their bewildered revenge from a different room entirely. Who was it?

- Ulysses either acted up at 11pm or swept a mug onto the floor – but not both
- Ralph had neither acted out of love nor gall
- The mug was not swiped as an act of vitriol
- Whoever had been overcome with gall had done so at 2am
- Cassini was feeling vitriolic
- The jewellery was not swiped at 3am
- 3am was not Ralph's time of mischief
- The jewellery swiper had not acted out of impertinence
- Ulysses swept the clock onto the floor

		Item				Reason				Time			
		Clock	Jewellery	Mug	Phone	Gall	Impertinence	Love	Vitriol	11pm	2am	3am	Midnight
Cat	Cassini												
	Hairy Claire												
	Ralph												
	Ulysses												
Time	11pm												
	2am												
	3am												
	Midnight												
Reason	Gall												
	Impertinence												
	Love												
	Vitriol												

Cat	Item	Time	Reason

64. Taste Test

Wilma, Rocco, Carnelian and Sister Maria von Cat had all planned to settle down for a cosy afternoon indoors while a storm raged outside. Their owners have just made themselves a nice hot drink in their favourite mugs, and human and cat have planned a snuggly nap on the sofa. That won't be happening now, however, as all four cats plunged one of their body parts into the hot drink as soon as it was put down, bringing the comfy and collegiate atmosphere to a swift close.

The cats immediately responded with a long, exceptionally penetrating yowl – but they have all evaded physical injury. The only injury is to their pride, as they have now been evicted from their respective cosy zones, and will have to spend the afternoon in exile.

Work out which cat interfered with what hot drink, in which mug, and what body part they dunked into it.

The cat who dipped their tail in the drink also made a special effort to sit on the freshly-baked cookie which had been set down to accompany it. Who was it?

- The hot chocolate was not in the mug adorned with fruit
- The spotty mug was intercepted by Carnelian
- The breakfast tea either had a nose or a tail dunked into it
- The breakfast tea was either Rocco's target or was in a fruity mug – but not both
- The drink in the striped mug didn't have a tongue dipped into it
- Wilma briefly infused herself in a mint tea
- Carnelian did not get involved with the hot chocolate
- The fruit mug either had a paw plopped into it or a part of Carnelian's body – but not both
- The hot chocolate was either contaminated with a paw or with a tongue
- The coffee either had a nose dipped into it or one of Carnelian's body parts – but not both

		Drink				Body part				Mug pattern			
		Breakfast tea	Coffee	Hot chocolate	Mint tea	Nose	Paw	Tail	Tongue	Flowers	Fruit	Spots	Stripes
Cat	Carnelian												
	Rocco												
	Sister Maria von Cat												
	Wilma												
Mug pattern	Flowers												
	Fruit												
	Spots												
	Stripes												
Body part	Nose												
	Paw												
	Tail												
	Tongue												

Cat	Drink	Mug pattern	Body part

65. Take a Seat

Xanthe, Saga, Odessa and Smooth Sammy live in perfect harmony with their owners, mainly because they are happy to cause untold chaos if it means they can get their own way. Today, the cats have decided to occupy the seat they knew very well that their owners were about to sit in, and have thus vetoed the activity their owner had planned to undertake while sitting in said chair.

The cats were all eventually coaxed out of their positions with careful attempts at flattery and successful offerings of treats – or so their owners thought. In fact, the cats have all slunk off to commit other crimes elsewhere in the house, fully of their own volition. No rest for the wicked, as they say.

Work out which cat stopped which planned activity, where their stolen seat was located, and what they subsequently slunk off to do later.

The cat who destroyed the toilet roll ate a few pieces of it as part of a social experiment, and will need to be whisked off to the vet. Who was it?

- Neither the conservatory nor the kitchen was the place where the howling cat had tried to sit
- The kitchen was either Smooth Sammy's ideal spot, or was favoured by the cat who went off to raid the bins – but not both
- Either Odessa prevented her owner from reading, or she ran off to chew some cables – but not both of these
- Xanthe was not the garden chair thief
- None of the owners had planned to send emails in their conservatory
- Whoever was evicted from the garden subsequently decided to raid some bins
- Saga had tried to steal a chair in either the living room or the kitchen
- Whoever destroyed the toilet roll hadn't delayed the sending of emails
- The person who wanted to watch the movie was either Saga's owner or had been planning to do so in the garden – but not both

		Planned activity				Additional crime				Location			
		Knitting	Reading	Sending emails	Watching a movie	Chewing cables	Destroying toilet roll	Howling	Raiding bins	Conservatory	Garden	Kitchen	Living room
Cat	Odessa												
	Saga												
	Smooth Sammy												
	Xanthe												
Location	Conservatory												
	Garden												
	Kitchen												
	Living room												
Additional crime	Chewing cables												
	Destroying toilet roll												
	Howling												
	Raiding bins												

Cat	Planned activity	Location	Additional crime

66. Sibling Rivalry

Yvonne, Pertinax, Harry and Sandra the Sassmeister have all been forced to endure the worst punishment any cat can be subjected to: living with their sibling. All four cats are comfortably more malicious than their much-maligned kin, who are constantly subjected to bouts of bullying, harassment and downright lunacy.

Today, the four devious cats have each come up with a new way to wind up their unsuspecting sibling, all of which will ensure maximum annoyance and disquiet. All four cats will be punished for their actions, but their general indifference to, and disrespect of, authority will ensure that their respective egos remain entirely intact.

Work out which cat bullied which sibling, what crime they committed against them, and what their punishment was.

The cat who blocked the cat flap to prevent their sibling entering the premises only did so when they thought their owner wasn't looking, for maximum deviousness. Who was it?

- Pertinax was not Lisa's sibling
- Yvonne bit her sibling
- Humphrey's tormentor was punished with no cuddles
- Lisa hadn't been bitten by her sibling
- The cat who blocked the cat flap was punished neither with tutting nor the removal of cuddles
- Claude was not Pertinax's long-suffering sibling
- The cat punished with no cuddles had either been lashing out or was Pertinax – but not both
- Either way, Harry wasn't the cat subjected to no cuddles as a punishment
- Harry hadn't tipped his sibling's water over
- Either Pertinax blocked the cat flap or was punished with banishment – but not both

		Sibling				Punish-ment				Crime			
		Blossom	Claude	Humphrey	Lisa	Banishment	Harsh words	No cuddles	Tutting	Biting	Blocking cat flap	Lashing out	Tipping water over
Cat	Harry												
	Pertinax												
	Sandra the Sassmeister												
	Yvonne												
Crime	Biting												
	Blocking cat flap												
	Lashing out												
	Tipping water over												
Punish-ment	Banishment												
	Harsh words												
	No cuddles												
	Tutting												

Cat	Sibling	Crime	Punishment

67. The Fall of Cat

Zelia, River, Sonny Bill and Her Royal Highness are such chaotic pets that, even in their absence, they can be responsible for untold mayhem. The four cats have decided to settle in for some uncharacteristic quiet time, which has caused their owners to worry that they are lost. In fact, the kitties have simply decided to curl up on top of an item of furniture so tall that it hides them entirely from view.

Concerned for their whereabouts, their owners have spent literal hours trying to hunt down the pets, who have been observing the chaos from on high. The cats will eventually jump down from their hiding spots and act like nothing has happened, though they will be secretly thrilled to have been the cause of so much attention and fuss.

Work out which cat hid in which location, how long their owner spent looking for them, and their eventual reason for descending from their elevated vantage point.

The cat who hid up the chimney briefly became stuck up there, but would never reveal this to anyone else as a matter of personal pride. Who was it?

- River was either searched for for exactly two hours or experienced malaise – but not both
- The cat in the chimney did not descend because of thirst
- Malaise was not the complaint of the cat atop the kitchen cupboard
- The cat on the kitchen cupboard, however, was sought for exactly four hours
- The cat on top of the refrigerator was searched for for more than two hours but fewer than five hours
- The cat searched for for exactly two hours did not reappear because of lonesomeness
- The cat who returned out of famishment had been the subject of a three-hour hunt
- Sonny Bill was not the cat searched for for exactly three hours
- Zelia eventually felt feelings of malaise

		High place				Reason for descent				Time spent looking			
		Chimney	Kitchen cupboard	Refrigerator	Wardrobe	Famishment	Lonesomeness	Malaise	Thirst	2 hours	3 hours	4 hours	5 hours
Cat	Her Royal Highness												
	River												
	Sonny Bill												
	Zelia												
Time spent looking	2 hours												
	3 hours												
	4 hours												
	5 hours												
Reason for descent	Famishment												
	Lonesomeness												
	Malaise												
	Thirst												

Cat	High place	Time spent looking	Reason for descent

68. Technically, No

Pomona, Valkyrie, Linda and Ethelred the Unruly are usually reasonable cats, but even they have their limits. Today, their owners have decided to selfishly ignore the cats for several minutes at a time, while they try to complete administrative tasks – and even in one case to just relax. The cats have a natural disposition for actively registering their discontent, and so have pulled out the cables powering the four devices which their owners had been using.

The cats' motivations for doing so did vary slightly in nuance, but the results were all the same: the immediate cessation of the activity which had briefly (and unacceptably) distracted their owners. Not satisfied when their owners simply plugged the devices back in, the cats decided to register their rage in a more obvious way: with incessant vocal expression.

Work out which cat unplugged what item, their reason for doing so, and the way in which they subsequently interrupted their owner.

The cat who unplugged the telephone had, in fact, already been meowing so loudly that the ongoing conversation was near useless anyway. Who was it?

- The phone was unplugged either by Ethelred the Unruly or by Linda
- Ethelred the Unruly indulged in a spot of crying
- The cat who pulled out the internet router was not the one who began whining
- The television cable was pulled out either by the whining cat or by Pomona – but not both
- The computer cords were pulled at out of tomfoolery – nothing more, nothing less
- Pomona had not acted out of frustration
- The cat who acted out of frustration was not the one who resorted to whining
- Linda had not acted out of tomfoolery, and nor had she been the one to unplug the phone
- The cat who ended up wailing had unplugged something either out of hostility or out of frustration
- Valkyrie's vocal protest consisted of bawling

		Unplugged item: Computer	Unplugged item: Internet router	Unplugged item: Phone	Unplugged item: Television	Interruption: Bawling	Interruption: Crying	Interruption: Wailing	Interruption: Whining	Reason: Frustration	Reason: Hostility	Reason: Rancour	Reason: Tomfoolery
Cat	Ethelred the Unruly												
	Linda												
	Pomona												
	Valkyrie												
Reason	Frustration												
	Hostility												
	Rancour												
	Tomfoolery												
Interruption	Bawling												
	Crying												
	Wailing												
	Whining												

Cat	Unplugged item	Reason	Interruption

69. A Quick Dip

Bob, Phinnaeus, Sir KitKat and The Duke of Cuddles are all adventurous cats, who love to explore the great outdoors and try new things. Unfortunately, their spirit of adventure is not matched with a natural agility, and all four cats have just lost their balance whilst trying to explore somewhere high up. The cats have met no physical peril because they have each fallen safely into a body of water, ensuring no lasting damage.

The cats may not be harmed in body, but these four cats detest swimming, whether the dip is planned or not. To cheer themselves up, the cats have all decided to indulge in a spot of hunting, and will take a live animal back to their bemused owners later on, proud of their ability to turn their luck around.

The cat that fell into a fountain will later try imitating its spraying action on a neighbour's door. Who was it?

- The cat who brought back a dormouse fell off either a statue or a fence
- The bee-bringer had fallen off a roof and into a lake
- Sir KitKat fell off a wall, though he wasn't the cat to subsequently bring back a bird
- Whoever fell into the paddling pool later brought back a cricket
- Bob either fell off a roof or brought back a bird – but not both
- Phinnaeus did not fall into the fountain, and nor had he fallen from a roof
- The fountain-bound cat was not the one who brought back a bird
- The bringer of the dormouse had not fallen off a fence

		Fell off				Animal				Body of water			
		Fence	Roof	Statue	Wall	Bee	Bird	Cricket	Dormouse	Fountain	Lake	Paddling pool	Pond
Cat	Bob												
	Phinnaeus												
	Sir KitKat												
	The Duke of Cuddles												
Body of water	Fountain												
	Lake												
	Paddling pool												
	Pond												
Animal	Bee												
	Bird												
	Cricket												
	Dormouse												

Cat	Fell off	Body of water	Animal

70. Hairy Situation

Vera, Amaryllis, Roger and Freddie the Faithful have beautiful gleaming coats as a result of extensive self-care and grooming routines. The cats regularly shun the offer of being brushed by their adoring owners, opting instead to groom themselves the good old-fashioned way – by licking themselves clean.

All is not zen, however. Not only does this somehow not prevent the appearance of cat hairs all over the house, but it also forces their owners to confront the other downside of having such meticulously groomed cats: hairballs. Today, all four cats have thrown up a hairball in a deeply inconvenient location, though none of the four pampered pets seem to be feeling a shred of remorse for their actions.

Work out which cat has which colour fur, what surface they brought up their hairball onto, and their chief emotion immediately after doing so.

The cat who threw up onto the clean laundry will tread muddy paw prints directly onto the same items once they have been rewashed. Who was it?

- The cat feeling relieved was either Roger or the cat who ruined the clean laundry – but not both
- The black furball wasn't the one on the clean laundry
- Amaryllis wasn't the cat feeling contentment
- The suede shoes were ruined either by Vera or by Roger
- Roger did not produce a black furball, and neither did Vera
- The cat who deposited their hairball onto the new sofa did so with great satisfaction
- Freddie the Faithful had not committed his crimes against clean laundry
- Roger had produced a white furball
- The orange cat was not the one feeling contentment
- Relief was the chief emotion of the cat who had desecrated fresh bedding

		Fur colour				Emotion				Onto			
		Black	Grey	Orange	White	Contentment	Pride	Relief	Satisfaction	Clean laundry	Fresh bedding	New sofa	Suede shoes
Cat	Amaryllis												
	Freddie the Faithful												
	Roger												
	Vera												
Onto	Clean laundry												
	Fresh bedding												
	New sofa												
	Suede shoes												
Emotion	Contentment												
	Pride												
	Relief												
	Satisfaction												

Cat	Fur colour	Onto	Emotion

71. A Surprise Meeting

Dillon, Shelley, Xavier and Mistress McPaw have all been up to no good, and it shows. The main evidence is that the cats have all appeared from nowhere with feathers around their mouths – but no feathered friend in sight. The cats have, in fact, all smuggled an avian adversary into the house, and have hidden them from the view of their rightfully suspicious owner.

The cats have then had a relaxing afternoon kicking back and watching their owners frantically search the house, trying to find evidence of any birds inside the said house. Only the cats know the true hiding places, and, as such, they all have feelings of deep superiority and smugness.

Work out which cat was spotted with what feathers, where they have hidden their unlucky catch, and how they feel about it.

The cat who hid their bird between two pillows will miss the moment of discovery as they will be outside causing more terror in the neighbourhood. Who was it?

- The cat who was feeling triumphant had hidden their bird either behind the TV or between pillows
- The brown-feathered bird had been hidden on the sofa
- Shelley was not the cat feeling victorious
- Neither was Xavier acting victorious, and nor had he hidden his bird on the sofa
- Dillon's bird was neither on the sofa nor behind the TV
- Xavier's bird was not hidden behind the TV
- The bird behind the TV, however, had grey feathers
- The bird under the bed was white
- Mistress McPaw had not brought in a brown-feathered bird
- The cat who had hidden their bird between two pillows was feeling – and acting – somewhat power-crazed

		Feathers				Attitude				Location			
		Black	Brown	Grey	White	Mighty	Power-crazed	Triumphant	Victorious	Behind TV	Between pillows	On sofa	Under bed
Cat	Dillon												
	Mistress McPaw												
	Shelley												
	Xavier												
Location	Behind TV												
	Between pillows												
	On sofa												
	Under bed												
Attitude	Mighty												
	Power-crazed												
	Triumphant												
	Victorious												

Cat	Feathers	Location	Attitude

72. Supply and Demand

Katherine, Quincy, Pootles and The Chaos Queen are friendly cats, who love to hang out. They are particularly interested in undivided attention, and have therefore spent a good hour this morning trying to distract their owners, who have been attempting to work from home.

When the cats' first methods of attracting attention all failed, they each tried a second method – which was, in some cases, more aggressive and arguably less appealing. Nevertheless, the four kitty cats eventually got the attention they so craved, and naturally immediately responded as though their human friend had lost their mind and they had never been interested in them at all.

Work out which cat used what methods for their first and second attempts at attracting attention, and then what they did as soon as their wish was granted.

The cat who escaped at speed will later get stuck on the roof and interrupt another important business meeting as their owner tries to coax them down. Who was it?

- The Chaos Queen was not the cat who escaped at speed
- The cat who tried spitting as their second attempt either went on to glower or to escape at speed
- Nuzzling was soon followed up with biting
- The cat who responded with departure was not the one who had just been crying
- The cat who had first purred did not later resort to scowling
- The Chaos Queen tried spitting as her second method of communication
- Quincy started off with some unproblematic purring
- The cat who scratched first was not the one who ended up scowling
- Katherine hadn't tried biting as her second method, and nor had she tried screaming as her first method
- The purring was not followed by crying

		First method				Response				Second method			
		Nuzzling	Purring	Scratching	Screaming	Departure	Escape at speed	Glower	Scowl	Biting	Crying	Spitting	Yowling
Cat	Katherine												
	Pootles												
	Quincy												
	The Chaos Queen												
Second method	Biting												
	Crying												
	Spitting												
	Yowling												
Response	Departure												
	Escape at speed												
	Glower												
	Scowl												

Cat	First method	Second method	Response

73. Unhinged and Untethered

Cory, Miriam, Vanilla and Dame Scratcher have all been forced into the deep injustice of wearing a collar, which goes against their values as free spirits and general nuisances. Luckily, the cats have quickly discovered that their collars can be detached if they manipulate them correctly, which naturally they have spent several days attempting.

Despite the collars being personally designed for them, with both their safety and comfort in mind, the cats have all now mastered the art of removing them. The cats only wore their shackles for a few days each and their reasons for removing them varied according to each individual pet. Regardless, all four cats will take extremely good care to make sure their owners never make this ridiculous and humiliating mistake again.

Work out which cat had been given what colour collar, how long they wore it for in total, and their reason for finally taking it off.

The cat who abandoned the navy collar briefly used it as a weapon to bully another local cat, who had looked at them the wrong way. Who was it?

- Dame Scratcher either removed her collar after four days, or did so out of irascibility – but not both
- The cat who removed their collar after six days did not do so out of puzzlement, and nor was it Miriam
- The cat with the coral collar acted out of crankiness
- The navy collar was not Vanilla's, and neither was the violet one
- The collar removed after six days was either cerulean or navy
- The cat who removed their collar after exactly four days was overcome with crankiness
- Cory had his collar on for more than two days – and when he finally removed it, it was because of irascibility
- Miriam did not have the violet collar on

		Colour				Reason				Time			
		Cerulean	Coral	Navy	Violet	Crankiness	Irascibility	Puzzlement	Whimsy	2 days	3 days	4 days	6 days
Cat	Cory												
	Dame Scratcher												
	Miriam												
	Vanilla												
Time	2 days												
	3 days												
	4 days												
	6 days												
Reason	Crankiness												
	Irascibility												
	Puzzlement												
	Whimsy												

Cat	Colour	Time	Reason

74. Remotely Interested

Annabelle, Greta, Spangles and The Fluffball were all enjoying a cosy evening on the sofa with their human friends when they decided, for no reason other than menace, to bring the fun to an end. The pals had all been snuggled up watching the television when the cats seized the remote controls, pressed a random selection of buttons, and asserted dominance over some harmless leisure time.

The cats subsequently decided that, rather than allowing their owners to undo the effects of the remote-hogging, they would, in fact, sit on the device and refuse to move. They were only lured out of their stubborn mindset when bribed by their owners with a different reward – which was, of course, all in their master plan.

Work out which cat interrupted which television programme, what they used the remote to do, and how they were bribed out of their wicked ways.

The cat who turned off the TV was a repeat offender who knew exactly which buttons to press – both literal and metaphorical – to get their way. Who was it?

- Spangles did not turn off the show his owner was watching, and nor did he interfere with a nature show
- The muted show was either a history show or was muted by Spangles – but not both
- Greta was not bribed with a new toy
- The Fluffball either interrupted a comedy show or was bribed with a new toy – but not both
- The turned-off show was either a comedy show or was turned off by the cat bribed with cuddles – but not both
- The cat who interrupted the history programme was offered a treat
- Greta enacted a channel change, while Annabelle hit the mute button

		Programme				Bribe				Effect			
		Comedy	Cookery	History	Nature	Cuddles	Dinner	New toy	Treat	Channel change	Mute	Pause	Turn off
Cat	Annabelle												
	Greta												
	Spangles												
	The Fluffball												
Effect	Channel change												
	Mute												
	Pause												
	Turn off												
Bribe	Cuddles												
	Dinner												
	New toy												
	Treat												

Cat	Programme	Effect	Bribe

75. Master Criminals

Boris, Ryan, Teresa and Ursula the Unruly are, to put it simply, master criminals. Not content with causing chaos on a small scale, the four cats have all carried out a crime spree in one short afternoon, totalling three different crimes each. Their reputations precede them, and yet their respective owners are still surprised that so much pettiness can exist in one single, cute, cuddly (-looking) cat.

All four cats have taken a long look at their greatest hits and each decided on three crimes which will wind up their owners and neighbours in precisely the most annoying way. They have planned their chaos meticulously, and committed their crimes in a specific order to invoke maximum mayhem. Their owners will cry in frustration and reel in shock at the acrimonious antics – but they will still acquiesce to cuddle up with the kitties at bedtime, due to the inescapable bonds of unconditional love.

Work out which cat committed which three crimes, one after another.

The cat who escaped as part of their third crime will briefly consider coming back with a live toad upon their return but will – miraculously – think better of it. Who was it?

- The cat who brought in a bird as their first crime followed it up by destroying the carpet
- The cat who screamed incessantly is not the one who finally escaped
- Teresa did not sit on a laptop as her first crime
- Ursula the Unruly was not the cat who first threw up on some laundry, and nor did she eventually bite her owner
- The cat whose final crime was to bite their owner had either brought in a bird or sat on a laptop as their first crime
- Teresa is not the cat who escaped as their final wicked deed
- Boris did not unravel any knitting, and neither did Ryan
- Whoever unravelled the knitting was not the cat who first unrolled a toilet roll, and nor was it the cat who smashed a water glass as their third effort
- The cat who screamed incessantly for their second act was either Boris or the cat who unrolled the toilet roll – but not both
- The cat who sat on a laptop escalated their crimes by later smashing a water glass

		Crime 1				Crime 3				Crime 2			
		Brought in a bird	Sat on laptop	Threw up on laundry	Unrolled toilet roll	Bit owner	Escaped	Litter protest	Smashed water glass	Chased dog	Destroyed carpet	Screamed incessantly	Unravelled knitting
Cat	Boris												
	Ryan												
	Teresa												
	Ursula the Unruly												
Crime 2	Chased dog												
	Destroyed carpet												
	Screamed incessantly												
	Unravelled knitting												
Crime 3	Bit owner												
	Escaped												
	Litter protest												
	Smashed water glass												

Cat	Crime 1	Crime 2	Crime 3

Solutions

Caught Red-pawed

Solution 1

Cat	Pet	Retaliation
Annie the Anarchist	Dog	Smashed vase
Megan	Gecko	Pulled down curtains
Shania	Goldfish	Ran away

Solution 2

Cat	Location	Toy
Braun	Top of fridge	Bells
Claudio	Shoe rack	Feather
Madam MacAdams	Bathtub	Scratch post

Solution 3

Cat	Notification	Activity
Adrian	Meowing	Chase butterflies
Emerald	Scratching door	Dig up vegetables
Lady Puffball	Headbutting door	Be a general menace

Solution 4

Cat	Body part	Soothing extra
Mini Minnie	Head	Purring
Saoirse	Toes	Nuzzling
Velma	Elbows	Cuddling

Solution 5

Cat	Food	Motive
Hermione	Spaghetti	Boredom
Lionel Scritchie	Irish stew	Spite
Tycho	Roast lamb	Insouciance

Solution 6

Cat	Reaction	Vegetable
Angelica	Hissing	Cucumber
Forrest	Spitting	Runner bean
Tortoiseshell Tim	Yelping	Broccoli

Solution 7

Cat	Number of storeys	Reaction
Cecily	5	Nonchalant
Indiana	7	Unconcerned
Meredith Blake	12	Defiant

Solution 8

Cat	Clothing	Hair colour
Calypso	Dress shirt	Grey
Cindy Clawford	Pyjamas	Ginger
Savannah	Y-fronts	Black

Solution 9

Cat	Hiding spot	Food
Cormac	Laundry basket	Tuna
Dr Watson	Bread bin	Salmon
Flash	Behind TV	Chicken

Solution 10

Cat	Location	Task
Lorelei	Bathroom	Important phone call
Pebbles	Office	Signing mortgage deeds
Spotty Simone	Kitchen	Treating minor injury

Solution 11

Cat	Entrance	Evidence
Gabriel	Window	Meow
The Whiskered Wonder	Door	Knocked over plant pot
Topaz	Cat flap	Hairs everywhere

Solution 12

Cat	Communication	Feelings
Maura	Yowling	Concern
Raddix	Whining	Disappointment
The Enigma	Crying	Desolation

Solution 13

Cat	Exile	Emotion
Catchu Picchu	Kitchen	Surprise
Storm	Bathroom	Disappointment
Vance	Living room	Defiance

Solution 14

Cat	Cupboard	Time spent
Asterix	Coat closet	1 hour
Catterin the Great	Pantry	2 hours
Baroness Bertha	Laundry cupboard	30 minutes

Solution 15

Cat	Insect	Evidence
Knox	Bumblebee	Wing
Madonna	Grasshopper	Leg
Quickstep Sally	Cockroach	Antenna

Solution 16

Cat	Room	Destroyed item
Crystal	Bathroom	Bathrobe
Fergal	Bedroom	Laptop
Nine Lives Lisa	Office	Soft cushion

Solution 17

Cat	Plant	Tool
Aqua	Sage	Hose
Lorenzo	Lavender	Rake
Mr Big	Rosemary	Spade

Solution 18

Cat	Kitten	Malicious act
Alexander Hameowlton	Peaches	Staring contest
Ariel	Cloudberry	Headbutting
Cinnabar	Muffin	Catcalling

Solution 19

Cat	Time	Demand
Melody	Midnight	Cuddles
Sorrel	3am	Attention
The Princess of Everything	2am	Treats

Solution 20

Cat	Pattern	Plates smashed
Dainty Dido	Checked	10
Esther	Striped	6
Marigold	Plain	9

Solution 21

Cat	Broken item	Additional symptom
Harry Houdini	Vase	Intense staring
Poppy	Television	Turbo-purring
Sapphire	Lamp	Tail chasing

Solution 22

Cat	Call with	Language
Dwight	Bank	Spanish
Moses	New job	Japanese
Professor Nibbles	Doctor's office	Norwegian

Solution 23

Cat	Instrument	Feeling
Asher	Piano	Perturbation
Butch Cassidy	Guitar	Triumphalism
Elektra	Violin	Jubilation

Solution 24

Cat	Notification	Follow-up activity
Aurora	Nuzzling	Ripping up carpet
Cosmic Craig	Yowling	Chasing dust
Gemma	Purring	Chewing slippers

Solution 25

Cat	Laundry state	Chewed item
Howard	Dry	Underpants
Maximus	Just-washed	Pyjamas
Rambo the Rogue	Unwashed	Woollen jumper

Solution 26

Cat	Door	Dinner ignored	Animal
Linford	Front	Fish	Frog
Sneaky St James	Back	Chicken	Bat
Truman	Side	Beef	Bird

Solution 27

Cat	Body part	Response	Object
Amanda	Ear	Hissing	TV remote
Billie Jean	Nose	Biting	Water jug
Dame Delilah	Tail	Swiping claws	Feather cushion

Solution 28

Cat	Dispensed item	Barrier	Room
Chucky	Ice cubes	Kitchen foil	Bedroom
Shannon	Crushed ice	Large sponge	Garage
Signora la Floof	Water	Sticky tape	Utility room

Solution 29

Cat	Injured area	Blanket pieces	Response to vet
Chicago	Front paw	4	Threw up on
Edgar Allan Paw	Ear	2	Scratched
Madeleine	Belly	6	Headbutted

Solution 30

Cat	Colour	Emotion	Play duration
Hebe	Orange	Shock	5 minutes
Maestro Max	Green	Distress	15 minutes
Sorcha	Yellow	Amusement	10 minutes

Solution 31

Cat	Pattern	Time of night	Object
Blossom	Lemons	3am	Shampoo bottle
Ripley	Waves	Midnight	Nail brush
The Prince of Darkness	Suns	1am	Radio

Solution 32

Cat	Bauble colour	Tinsel colour	Berries
Carol	Green	Gold	Ivy
Isambard	Blue	Silver	Holly
Mysterious Clive	Pink	White	Mistletoe

Solution 33

Cat	Dog name	Dog colour	Attitude
Callum	Rory	Black	Smug
Lawless Larry	Max	Gold	Hubristic
Santiago	Spike	Brown	Imperious

Solution 34

Cat	Book cover	Liquid	Demand
Isa	Red	Water	Attention
Mrs Snuggleton	Purple	Tea	Food
Olive	Green	Juice	Freedom

Solution 35

Cat	Scent	Addition	Dangerous item
Eugene	Lavender	Bubbles	Candle
Keanu	Ginger	Bath salts	Razor
The Amazing Abigail	Coconut	Bath bomb	Medicine

Solution 36

Cat	Blind material	Sparkly object	People woken
Magdalena	Cloth	Street light	3
Malcolm the Majestic	Metal	Moon	5
Phoenix	Wood	Aeroplane	1

Solution 37

Cat	Dish	Reason	Banished to
Cosima	Spaghetti	Clumsiness	Outside
Evander	Casserole	Spite	Hallway
Princess Peach	Soup	Curiosity	Living room

Solution 38

Cat	Item	Material	Colour
Bubbles	Coat	Wool	Mauve
Calamity Jane	Trousers	Linen	Mustard
Sophie	Shirt	Cotton	Mulberry

Solution 39

Cat	Cable colour	Device	Untangling time
JackJack	Black	TV	30 mins
Lois Lane	Silver	Vacuum cleaner	20 mins
Mystique	Red	Heater	45 mins

Solution 40

Cat	Victim cat	Perceived offence	Gardens chased through
Royce	Pom Pom	Staring	4
Simon the Stripey	Melon	Existing	7
Sydney	Loopy	Trespassing	5

Solution 41

Cat	Item	Location	Notification
Crusoe	Yoghurt pot	Toilet bowl	Screaming
Llewellyn	Used diaper	Kitchen table	Purring
Mike the Magician	Banana peel	Front doormat	Meowing

Solution 42

Cat	Number of swipes	Toy	Chief emotion
Jane Pawsten	12	Feather duster	Abhorrence
Lancelot	5	Squeaky mouse	Revulsion
Maia	9	Fluffy bunny	Loathing

Solution 43

Cat	Time	Motive	Days banished
Maurice	1am	Ennui	4 days
Sirius	3am	Caprice	8 days
The Lion King	5am	Loneliness	6 days

Solution 44

Cat	Cat's supper	Dog's supper	Dog's name
Fleur	Mackerel	Beef	Barry
Kylo	Prawns	Turkey	Clive
Little Miss Fluff	Tuna	Pork	Maureen

Solution 45

Cat	Feeling	Call	Time
Ezra	Petulance	Job interview	3 minutes
Griffin	Existential dread	Mortgage application	4 minutes
Major Mischief	Cantankerousness	Credit card company	8 minutes

Solution 46

Cat	Bird	Hiding place
Paloma	Magpie	Shoe cupboard
Sandy Claws	Tit	Pantry
Serena	Robin	Downstairs toilet
Titus	Wren	Porch

Solution 47

Cat	Body part	Reason
Calvin	Hand	Malice
Daisy	Toe	Inquisitiveness
Halo	Nose	Hostility
Officer Snuggles	Knee	Affection

Solution 48

Cat	Food demanded	Response
Drew	Cod	Slow blinking
Earl	Chicken	Screaming
Neptune	Duck	Walking away
The Void	Sardines	Biting ankles

Solution 49

Cat	Guessed reason	Secret crime
Agnes	Entertainment	Brought in mouse
Catriona	Friendship	Chewed shoe
Saint	Incorrigibility	Destroyed toilet roll
The Escape Artist	Love	Unravelled jumper

Solution 50

Cat	Toy ignored	Preferred object
Achilles	Scratching post	Toothbrush
Jacqueline	Personal yurt	Mop head
Lennox	Ball with bell	Salt shaker
The Mousetrap	Rubber fish	Throw cushion

Solution 51

Cat	Reason	Time on roof
Callisto	Stalking bird	3 hours
Dylan	Better view	2 hours
Jeffery	Not paying attention	5 hours
Shambolic Steve	Sunbathing	6 hours

Solution 52

Cat	Furniture	Motive
Finn	Armchair	Vindictiveness
Jennifer	Footstool	Experimentation
The Boss	Laundry basket	Listlessness
Troy	Nightstand	Research

Solution 53

Cat	Method	Animal
Evan	Smashing water glass	Toad
Jericho	Sitting on face	Rat
Nero	Ceaseless screaming	Vole
Prue the Prancer	Setting off alarm	Grasshopper

Solution 54

Cat	Planned activity	Attitude
Andromeda	Making enemies	Indifference
Captain Chaos	Being a menace	Flippancy
Chelsea	Terrorizing neighbours	Jauntiness
Jade	Inspiring fear	Nonchalance

Solution 55

Cat	Favourite word	Demand
Ajax	Treat	Food
Edgar	Bedtime	Attention
Emma the Brave	Dindins	Cuddles
Jolene	Fluffy	Grooming

Solution 56

Cat	Activity interrupted	Secondary crime
Chief Ratter	Work call	Litter protest
Dalloway	Laundry administration	Climbing on curtains
Frances	Cleaning	Smashing glasses
Juniper	Nap	Eating socks

Solution 57

Cat	Food	Plate
Aeneas	Jacket potato	China
Colonel Mouser	Pasta bake	Porcelain
Hilary	Chicken bagel	Stoneware
Jeepers	Lamb curry	Glass

Solution 58

Cat	Perceived reason	Actual reason
Idina	Distress	Tedium
Muriel	Loneliness	Mischief
Neo	Hunger	Impishness
Ray the Rioter	Anxiety	Devilment

Solution 59

Cat	House number	Hiding place
Disgraceful Grace	11	Recycling bin
Isaac	4	Kitchen table
Lysander	13	Dog's bed
Opal	25	Shoe rack

Solution 60

Cat	Communication method	Room
Disorderly Derek	Nudging	Kitchen
Enya	Chirping	Living room
Newton	Intense staring	Bathroom
Orla	Whining	Garage

Solution 61

Cat	Reason	Treat	Activity
Empurror Julius	Vacation	Catnip	Sulking
Orville	Vet visit	Chicken	Howling
Pamela	House move	Trout	Plotting
Paris	Emergency	Salmon	Seething

Solution 62

Cat	Attitude	New cat	Item
Inigo the Interrupter	Offended	Mina	Water bowl
Philomena	Resentful	Scamp	Scratching post
Reagan	Affronted	Polka Dot	Window seat
Zenith	Disgusted	Jinx	Litter tray

Solution 63

Cat	Item	Time	Reason
Cassini	Phone	3am	Vitriol
Hairy Claire	Jewellery	2am	Gall
Ralph	Mug	Midnight	Impertinence
Ulysses	Clock	11pm	Love

Solution 64

Cat	Drink	Mug pattern	Body part
Carnelian	Coffee	Spots	Tail
Rocco	Breakfast tea	Stripes	Nose
Sister Maria von Cat	Hot chocolate	Flowers	Tongue
Wilma	Mint tea	Fruit	Paw

Solution 65

Cat	Planned activity	Location	Additional crime
Odessa	Reading	Garden	Raiding bins
Saga	Watching a movie	Living room	Howling
Smooth Sammy	Sending emails	Kitchen	Chewing cables
Xanthe	Knitting	Conservatory	Destroying toilet roll

Solution 66

Cat	Sibling	Crime	Punishment
Harry	Lisa	Blocking cat flap	Harsh words
Pertinax	Blossom	Tipping water over	Banishment
Sandra the Sassmeister	Humphrey	Lashing out	No cuddles
Yvonne	Claude	Biting	Tutting

Solution 67

Cat	High place	Time spent looking	Reason for descent
Her Royal Highness	Refrigerator	3 hours	Famishment
River	Wardrobe	2 hours	Thirst
Sonny Bill	Kitchen cupboard	4 hours	Lonesomeness
Zelia	Chimney	5 hours	Malaise

Solution 68

Cat	Unplugged item	Reason	Interruption
Ethelred the Unruly	Phone	Frustration	Crying
Linda	Television	Rancour	Whining
Pomona	Internet router	Hostility	Wailing
Valkyrie	Computer	Tomfoolery	Bawling

Solution 69

Cat	Fell off	Body of water	Animal
Bob	Roof	Lake	Bee
Phinnaeus	Fence	Pond	Bird
Sir KitKat	Wall	Paddling pool	Cricket
The Duke of Cuddles	Statue	Fountain	Dormouse

Solution 70

Cat	Fur colour	Onto	Emotion
Amaryllis	Orange	Clean laundry	Pride
Freddie the Faithful	Black	New sofa	Satisfaction
Roger	White	Fresh bedding	Relief
Vera	Grey	Suede shoes	Contentment

Solution 71

Cat	Feathers	Location	Attitude
Dillon	White	Under bed	Victorious
Mistress McPaw	Grey	Behind TV	Triumphant
Shelley	Brown	On sofa	Mighty
Xavier	Black	Between pillows	Power-crazed

Solution 72

Cat	First method	Second method	Response
Katherine	Scratching	Crying	Escape at speed
Pootles	Nuzzling	Biting	Scowl
Quincy	Purring	Yowling	Departure
The Chaos Queen	Screaming	Spitting	Glower

Solution 73

Cat	Colour	Time	Reason
Cory	Violet	3 days	Irascibility
Dame Scratcher	Coral	4 days	Crankiness
Miriam	Navy	2 days	Puzzlement
Vanilla	Cerulean	6 days	Whimsy

Solution 74

Cat	Programme	Effect	Bribe
Annabelle	History	Mute	Treat
Greta	Nature	Channel change	Cuddles
Spangles	Cookery	Pause	New toy
The Fluffball	Comedy	Turn off	Dinner

Solution 75

Cat	Crime 1	Crime 2	Crime 3
Boris	Sat on laptop	Screamed incessantly	Smashed water glass
Ryan	Brought in a bird	Destroyed carpet	Bit owner
Teresa	Threw up on laundry	Unravelled knitting	Litter protest
Ursula the Unruly	Unrolled toilet roll	Chased dog	Escaped

Also available from the same authors:

Meowdle: 75 Feline Crime Puzzles to Solve Using Logic, Skill and the Power of Catnip

ISBN 978-1-52944-200-7

Woofdle: 75 Canine Crime Puzzles to Solve Using Logic, Skill & the Power of Walkies

ISBN 978-1-52944-779-8